THE GHOST
The Davis Order
THE BEGINNING

A NOTE FROM THE AUTHOR

ALL MY BOOKS ARE UNIQUE TO THEIR MAIN CHARACTERS. They write the story; I'm just along for the ride. They make mistakes that can have you either relate to, like, or dislike (possibly even hate) them. They are raw and flawed, but we love them anyway.

Important for this Novella:

*THE **GHOST*** IS George's story. If you have read ***The Dark Series*** or ***Davis Order***, you met or heard of him as an adult. If this is your introduction to my world(s), you are in for a wild ride.

GEORGE'S NOVELLA gives you his backstory, as well as serves as an introduction to my series.

The Ghost is fast-paced and split into two parts: past and present. The past covers George's twenties, after he arrives home from college, and is set in the early to mid-nineties. The prologue and present chapters span multiple books of **The Dark Series** and **Davis Order**. **Each present chapter identifies which book in the series time line it falls into.**

WHILE GEORGE GETS **his happily ever after, not everything is concluded or answered in this novella. I promise that you will get your answers in my books.** Which ones? That's once again up to the characters. I included a short glossary at the end of this novella for all the characters you will encounter and where you will see them next or what their story is.

IF YOU HAVE READ my previous books, you are familiar with my writing and how I thrive on the small details. However, *The Ghost* is a novella, which meant I had to cut the "fluffy filler scenes." A lot of them. If you notice jumps in the story, that is why.

All the mentioned regions, sites, and locations you encounter in this book are fictional to fit the story.

It is **not necessary** to read **The Dark Series** or **Davis Order** before **The Ghost,** but you will want to dive in after you get a taste of these worlds.

The Ghost is intended for **MATURE (18+)** readers. It is a dark, forbidden, second-chance novella and features strong language, violence, explicit sexual scenes, and situations that may be considered **TRIGGERS** for some. **Reader discretion is advised.**

(For a more detailed list of potential triggers and tropes in this book, click here or scan the below QR code.)

Mary, this one is for you.
You knew that there was more to George before I finished writing Out of
the Dark. I'll forever be grateful for your friendship, PA support, and
everything in between. To many more books together.

To listen to *George and Lou's* playlist on Spotify, scan the below barcode.

PROLOGUE

GEORGE

Time line:

Out of the Dark (The Dark Series, Book Two)
George's perspective as he gets introduced to everyone.

THE TIGHTNESS in my throat is another new (*and old*) sensation I'm not used to anymore. I lost my ability to feel. I didn't need it. My job was to handle the security. Yet, morality still lived in my bones. While I took care of everyone's mistakes, I couldn't turn them in. Who was I to judge? I was playing the long game, after all.

But lately, all kinds of memories and, with that, emotions have resurfaced. Emotions I buried nearly twenty-five years ago —when she became a Davis.

That was the day I became *The Ghost*.

. . .

STANDING IN THE DARK, I watch Rhys McGuire mourn his missed opportunity to speak to his girlfriend. I know where she is, but he doesn't. His friends want to comfort him, but their postures reveal their inability to do so. None of this is surprising. What do three eighteen-ish-year-old children know about the cruel reality of society? A world where criminals hide in plain sight with a throne that was meant to be mine.

I LISTEN to their conversation as they sit around the firepit on the Kellers' back patio.

"What happened?" Weston Sheats inquires with a subdued tone. I observed him to be the comedian of the group, not to be taken seriously.

"Kat," Rhys McGuire elaborates, but of course, it doesn't make sense to his friends.

I shift to my other foot. It's almost time.

"Come again?" Denielle Keller's shocked expression nearly elicits a laugh.

A laugh. Huh.

"Kat happened." Rhys breathes raggedly. "I don't know what to do."

It's time.

"Maybe I can help with that." Using my voice, breathing normally after hiding in the dark for so long, lifts the pressure off my chest.

Three sets of eyes jerk in my direction, searching the bushes surrounding the patio.

I step into the light.

"HOLY FUCK!" Weston shouts and falls off his chair.

Denielle Keller screams, and Rhys just stares at me.

Part One

The Order.

CHAPTER ONE

GEORGE

PAST

"G. It's about time you show your ugly face again."

I slap my best friend on the back. "Maybe you should try college sometime, asshole." Forcing the corners of my mouth up, the expression feels like a sneer on my face. After four years away, I should be happy to be home, yet a hollow void had steadily spread from behind my ribs through every part of my body the closer our private jet got to New York.

There was a reason I decided to go to school overseas.

Meeting him at *Underworld,* his family's club, was the last thing I wanted after hours of traveling, but he didn't give me a choice. Marshall Davis never does.

My eardrums vibrate from the near-concussive bass as Daft Punk's "Around the World" pounds out of the speakers from the floor below. Davis lights one of his signature Silk Cuts. My fingers twitch with the urge to snatch it from his grasp and drown it in his tumbler. The stench violates my nose and burns its way to my lungs. I peer around the VIP lounge for a waitress. I need a drink to swallow down the ashy taste. We don't mingle with the *Norms*. The upstairs of the club is reserved for invite only. Not even the New Yorker elite make it past the black velvet rope if Davis doesn't allow it.

Davis takes another drag. He doesn't touch his father's merchandise but lights up at every opportunity—which is always. Walter Davis's philosophy of *never sample what you sell* has had his son brainwashed since diapers. Davis Senior would force the powder up one's nose at gunpoint, but heaven forbid his son dare take it.

My friend's family is more fucked up than mine. But that's why the Davises and Weilers are two of the three families making up the council of *The Order*. Our families are ruthless and don't take prisoners. You're either part of it, or...you're dead.

"Eh, I don't need a degree for where I'm going." He waves his cancer stick through the air. "Let's check out the pussy for the night. I need to get my cock sucked." His leering grin sends chills down my spine.

I crack my thumb with my curled fingers. His crude remark summarizes his opinion of women. One day, one of them will cut his dick off.

We stride over the polished black marble floor to the railing, and my hands tighten around the cool metal. The skin over my knuckles burns as I roll my shoulders back, concentrating on loosening my grip.

I immediately know when Davis has found his mark. His chin lifts and he angles his head ever so slightly. To the untrained observer, he hasn't moved at all. But we've learned to read each other without making eye contact. Following his line of sight, I spot a *flock* of girls dancing together.

"Which one? Or are you in the mood for an orgy?" I drawl as if the thought didn't make me want to vomit. I'm the black sheep of *The Order*. I'm part of it, but at the same time, I'm not. I was born with a conscience.

"Not today." He throws back the amber liquid. "I think I'm in the mood for a tall one." He aims his finger at the girl while holding on to his now empty glass. His *prey* has dark hair and legs that appear endless—his usual type.

Turning behind him, Davis signals for one of his lackeys. "Go get 'em."

From the VIP area of the club, we can look down at everyone, but from below, all you see is the railing. What happens beyond that stays up here.

Dum-Dum approaches the group with confidence he should not have. He is literally Davis's bitch. But being part of *The Order*, in any capacity, gives these idiots the idea they have power.

What a fucking joke.

He gestures up, and several sets of eyes swivel in our direction. Davis salutes with his somehow refilled tumbler, but I'm rooted in place. Every cord in my body tenses as I hold the chocolate stare of Eloise Cartwright. Despite the club's dim atmosphere and strobe lights, I remember the warm color of her irises. The Cartwrights are part of our circle. I've seen her growing up but haven't been around her since leaving the country for college—when she was a senior in high school.

Holy fucking shit. She's stunning.

Something stirs inside of me, and I hold my breath. Eloise slants her head as if she's listening to my thoughts. Her gaze is curious and, at the same time, reserved and challenging.

One of her friends, whom I identify as Carolyn Veil, grabs her hand as they climb the stairs, and she finally breaks the connection.

Air exits my lungs with a whoosh, and I blink.

What the hell was that?

CHAPTER TWO

LOU

George Weiler is back. How did I not know he was home?

I follow Nic and Car, my eyes glued to the steps. Of course, today was the day I let them talk me into wearing heels. I didn't plan on doing more than standing at the bar, let alone climb into the lion's den of the devil, a.k.a. Marshall Davis. Everyone knows what goes on up here.

We reach the top and Marshall saunters toward us with his arms wide. "Ladies, welcome. I didn't expect to see you this fine evening."

Fine evening?

What the fuck is he on? No, his drug of choice is not the recreational kind. He indulges in a very different type of *high*.

With downstairs packed to max capacity, I'm surprised that most of the circular booths are unoccupied. He veers toward Nic, and Car stiffens. She has had her eye on the firstborn of the

Davises since...always. But when his father made the official announcement on his twentieth birthday that Marshall would take over in five years (as if this was any news), she became even more determined. For the last twenty-four months, my best friend has destroyed every girl just attempting to lay a finger on him. Not that this would change anything. But I'm not the one to rub it in her face. We're all in denial in one way or another.

I walk everyone farther into the lounge. The song switches to "Insomnia" by Faithless. Still not my preferred style of music, but better than the previous torture. While the entire club is open concept, the assault on my ears is not nearly as loud up here.

"Eloise Cartwright."

I close my eyes as he breathes my name, my hair tickling my bare shoulder. I didn't notice him approach from his spot at the railing as I was focused on the devil himself. Marshall already has my other best friend draped under his arm, leading her away.

Nic and I met in college and hit it off. While she was free-spirited and enjoyed the perks my status gave her, she was still new and not part of our inner circle.

I should keep Car company before she turns on Nic, but my body has a mind of its own. I pivot as gracefully as possible on my unwanted footwear and come nose to nose—literally—with one of New York's most desired bachelors.

George is known for many things—he is part of *The Order*, after all—but what has always intrigued me the most: he lacks the cruelty of his best friend. Being the same age, they were thrown together since birth. Yet, George doesn't disrespect or use women for his pleasure like Marshall. He had put his education first and would soon join the Marine Corps. While it was just part of the process, implanting himself into the field that served his family best for their business deals, I could see him being in the military.

"George Weiler. I didn't know you were back."

He arches a brow, the corner of his mouth twitching ever so slightly.

"I go by Lou these days." I place my palms on his corded forearms and a jolt of heat zips to my core. "I'm disappointed you didn't come to see me."

You never interacted more than a cordial hello. Why would he come to see you?

My toes curl inside their confinement while I'm waiting for him to laugh in my face. Instead, he surprises me.

"I just got back, *Lou*, but had I known you were waiting, I would have made you my priority." His large hands land on my hips, his fingers applying the slightest of pressure against the fabric of my dress. He might as well have burned his touch to my flesh.

My teeth sink into my bottom lip, and I watch his nostrils flare. His focus remains on my mouth, and the sudden urge to lick the seam of his lips overcomes me. My body buzzes with a craving I've never experienced before, and I slowly glide my fingers up his arms until I can intertwine them behind his neck.

George dips his head, aligning his cheek with mine. "What happened to the girl that wouldn't make eye contact with anyone?" His nose nudges the shell of my ear, and goose bumps rocket down my spine.

He remembers me. My heart rate picks up. But if from excitement or fear of what he'll do once he discovers that this girl doesn't exist anymore, I'm not sure. That part of me has remained behind the walls of the Institute ever since my first visit.

"She took her position early," I whisper, unable to hide the truth from him. George has a pull on me that makes no sense. A compulsion to let him see me—the real me. We grew up under the same rules, but some of us had more freedom than others. He had been able to leave this world—for a little while.

His spine stiffens, and he recoils. George searches my eyes, and I mesh my lips together.

He frames my face with his palms, his thumb stroking my cheekbone. "Define early."

The Cartwright branch of *The Order* runs an institution located outside of New York that specializes in reforming the unwilling—making them obey and follow the rules.

"Father has had me observing over the last two years, preparing for the takeover," I confess. George and I have a similar view of the world we were born into, yet I would eat my tongue before admitting that to anyone. I value being alive—not *my* life, per se, but having a pulse.

"Why this early?" George's narrowed eyes bleed with suspicion.

I shrug a shoulder. "Twenty is not that early in our world. What difference do a few years make?" Playing it off as if it isn't a big deal to torture and brainwash human beings into submission has become second nature—after I threw up my lunch the first time I witnessed the process. *We don't show weakness*—or empathy, as any sane person would call it—is my father's cardinal rule.

George caresses my cheek with his thumb. "*Mania*, don't think I don't see past your facade." The corner of his mouth lifts.

Mania, the spirit goddess of insanity, madness, crazed frenzy, and the dead—if that isn't an accurate description of who I am, or will be one day, as the firstborn Cartwright. *The Order* doesn't discriminate by gender. The firstborn takes over on their twenty-fifth birthday. Male or female.

With his nickname for me on his lips, I bridge the distance, feathering my mouth against his. George groans, and my boldness surprises me, but once the connection is made, every nerve ending in my body lights up like an inferno. I tighten my hold behind his head and draw closer until my breasts are flush with his defined chest. I swear I can feel his heart thunder in sync with mine.

What are we doing?

His initial hesitation melts away, and George slants his head, giving himself (and me) better access. My lips part, and he takes the invitation. Our tongues collide, and my lids snap shut. An electric current surges through me, and when his hands drop to my ass, I react on autopilot. My legs wrap around his midsection, forcing him to hold me up. With only a couple of steps, George walks us to one of the booths and sinks smoothly into the plush seat without the slightest sign of struggle from carrying my weight. He pulls me forward, and when my pussy grinds against his hard length, stars explode against the back of my lids. I moan into his mouth, but George suddenly breaks the connection. His eyes find mine, and his heaving chest betrays the shutters that just fell over his features.

I hold his blank gaze, understanding settling in. Peering to the side, I find Marshall watching us. His demeanor conveys disinterest. His arms are spread on either side of the seat, his jeans pooling at his ankles. Nic kneels between his legs, blowing him, and Car sucks on his neck like she's auditioning for *Interview with a Vampire*. He doesn't even attempt to be subtle about it. Why would he? We all grew up together. We are all pawns of the game. An unspoken threat burns in his stare, and while I want to take him up on the challenge, I avert my eyes. Finding George studying me, I let my manic mask fall into place.

I'm Mania.

"Let's go dance. I'm bored." Not that I want to. I'll probably break a freaking ankle. But I still slip off George's lap and pull on his hand, letting my words hover in the VIP area for everyone to hear. Car spares me a fleeting glance before continuing her exploration of Marshall's neck. Nic waves her hand without breaking stride in the head-bobbing department.

We're all just a bunch of depraved kids that grew up under even more depraved parents.

CHAPTER THREE

GEORGE

FOUR WEEKS AGO, I DANCED WITH LOU UNTIL THREE IN THE morning—something I'd never done before. I associate with the offspring of *The Order*, but at the same time, I don't—not the real me. She was different.

Every moment I'm not with my family, friends, or preparing to leave, my thoughts wander back to her body pressed against mine. She is the first image entering my consciousness when I wake up and the last when I lie in bed at night.

Her long blonde hair flowed around her as she had her arms over her head, dancing without a care in the world to the obnoxious music *Underground* drowned us in. I couldn't take my eyes off her. When the beat finally slowed, she let me draw her close without the slightest hesitation. My mind teetered on the verge of intoxication without the help of recreational substances. I hadn't touched my drink since we left the VIP lounge. Her radiant smile as she looked up at me sent a bolt of...*want*(?) through me. It was a need I could barely rein in. The only thing keeping me from dragging her off into the nearest dark corner—fuck, I didn't even care if it was dark—was the knowledge that my best friend was upstairs, probably watching us. We swayed to song after song. She asked me about college, what it was like to live in Europe for the past few years, and if I missed it. Did I? I thought I would—until I laid eyes on Lou. For the first time, I didn't want to board my father's jet again.

TONIGHT IS MY FAREWELL PARTY, and Penelope decided it had to be themed. I just patted her head and left after the announcement. When my little sister sets her mind to something, there is no talking her out of it.

Indulging her in her current '20s flapper obsession, I bust out our grandfather's three-piece pin-striped suit and fedora. Penny jumps up and down, clapping her hands like a lunatic when I exit my room. Her reaction is worth the uncomfortable outfit strangling my balls. She adored our grandfather before he passed a few years ago, but Grandfather was skinnier than me. While it fits everywhere else, that particular area does not.

"Guests arrive in thirty minutes." She beams, grabs me by the sleeve, and tugs. "Come on. I want to show you downstairs."

Reaching the front hall, I halt in my tracks. My stomach bottoms out as my eyes take everything in. I know she hired an event planner, but I didn't expect a prohibition speakeasy to have replaced the first floor of our home. I'm shocked Mother let her get away with that.

I LEAN with my elbow against the bar and watch the jazz band. Penny and Abigail are dancing in front of the makeshift stage, with every male waiting for their dresses to ride up another inch. Davis lounges next to me, observing our sisters with amusement.

"You gonna do something about those perverts ogling Penny?" He brings his tumbler to his lips, another Silk Cut between his fore- and middle finger.

"Are you?" I counter, flicking my eyes in his direction. He's the one everyone fears to piss off, not me.

He ponders my challenge. When a menacing smirk overtakes his expression, cold fingers choke me. I curse under my breath. I know that look.

Davis places his glass on the bar top and pushes off. My mouth goes dry, and I follow my best friend as he aims for a shorter guy I've seen before but have no clue what his name is. I gave Penny free rein with the guest list. I'm pretty sure he is somewhere on the payroll, but as to what or which family, I couldn't begin to guess.

His eyes bulge as it registers that he is the target of the devil. His gaze darts left and right, but his buddies have already scrambled as Davis latches on to his beefy neck.

"You like eye-fucking my sister?" Davis leans in. "Or should I ask her to strip for you so you actually can take a good look?" A red tint slowly slithers up the strangled idiot. I keep my face neutral as pity weighs me down.

What did he expect?

"I—uh— No, Marshall. I wasn't—" he stammers, but his pathetic attempt at an excuse is cut off by a guttural scream as Davis stubs out his cigarette in the poor schmuck's eye.

I wrinkle my nose as the stench fills the air.

Abigail and Penny appear next to us. Where my sister looks mortified, the second-born Davis props her fists on her glitter-covered hips.

"Really, Marsh? This is a party. You could've at least taken Donny outside. The whole room reeks now." Her exasperation at the unpleasant odor while Davis still has his hand wrapped around a whimpering *Donny's* throat makes bile coat my tongue.

My friend peers at his sister, lets the guy drop and reaches for his pack of smokes. "What a fucking waste of a cigarette." Stepping over the dude, who clutches his face, Davis doesn't attempt to avoid the hand Donny uses to prop himself up. The band stopped playing when Davis brought all the attention to him. A crunching sound reverberates through the room, and Donny howls but still doesn't move to leave.

Penny regards me with wide eyes, and I have to play my part. Rubbing my palm over my nose and mouth, I snap my finger at no one in particular. "Clean this up."

This. Him.

I can taste the burn on my tongue and fight the urge to spit.

Out of nowhere, two of my men appear, grab Donny under the arms, and haul him to his feet. With my hands in my pockets, pretending this whole scene didn't disgust me, I trail the threesome out the door.

Halting at the top steps, I see Lou, Nic, and Carolyn exit a cab in front of our brownstone.

The girls watch my guys deposit Davis's victim into the cab still idling at the curb.

Carolyn saunters up the stairs. "Marshall?" The unsurprised disinterest in her question makes me clench my teeth.

Lou's friend is as smart as she is cunning. She's been after Davis since high school, probably longer, and knows his temper best—aside from me. She wants to be at the top, and my best friend is her ticket to power. Unfortunately for her, she's not a firstborn and has to fall in line.

I give her my best bored look, not feeling like rehashing Davis's antics. It wasn't the first and won't be the last. Gesturing for them to come inside, Carolyn passes me without another glance. From the gossip Penny recapped to me after arriving home almost a month ago, Nic is their newest addition. Her wary steps betray her. Lou stops at my side, watching her friends disappear through the door.

She glances up, and suddenly everything is right again. "Mania."

"Ares," she counters, and my brows pop.

Greek mythology is a mandatory subject for everyone in *The Order*. Why? I never figured it out, but we are all taught the same. And *Ares* is the god of war—my family's role in *The Order*.

CHAPTER FOUR

LOU

After reliving the night in my head for weeks, I put on my big-girl panties and come to George's farewell party. I knew the day was coming.

Car was basically attached to Marshall's groin whenever he didn't have anyone else riding his dick. Marshall informed Car about George's departure, and Car relayed it to me.

The moment her words sank in, needles pricked in my throat. I shouldn't have had such a visceral reaction. Yes, I've known George all my life, but the night at *Underworld* changed everything. I no longer accept my position. I want more. I want...love. Love? It is too early to define the connection we formed in that way, yet deep down, the knowledge simmers that this is what we could have—if we were anyone else.

Seeing George at the top of the steps in his suit, a swarm of butterflies takes flight behind my ribs. The fluttery sensation spreads through every limb and settles where my panties should be. I've forgone underwear in favor of my dress.

Addressing him as the god of war feels right. Where I will rule the insane, he will be in charge of the artillery.

George runs his tongue along his teeth as his hungry gaze rakes over my body.

"You look stunning." He steps closer, and I wrap my fingers around the lapels of his jacket.

"You're not so bad yourself, Mr. Weiler." I tip my chin up. Holding his gaze, I drown in his near-black irises. I'm convinced I see specs of blue shimmering in the void. Were he anyone else, his eyes would make him appear pure evil.

George hovers his lips above mine. "I don't want to leave without another taste."

My breath hitches. "Then don't." I tighten my hold and pull him closer until our mouths connect.

It's a fleeting kiss, promising something I will never forget. As soon as it starts, it is already over, but the fire is fueled.

George interlaces our hands and pulls me inside. He bypasses the party, guiding me toward the stairs leading to the second floor. Out of the corner of my eye, I notice Car and Nic flanking Marshall—no surprise. What injects ice into my veins is Marshall's impassive stare on me.

I turn my head and keep my focus on George's back as we ascend. With every step, the cold melts, and the devil's hold loosens.

George aims for the third door on the right, and as soon as we're behind the wooden barrier, my back is pressed against a wall.

My arms wind around his neck as he brings our bodies flush. George's mouth comes down with a hungry force, eliciting a noise resembling a whimper in my throat. My heart thunders inside my chest, making me light-headed.

A click indicates that he has locked us in. His fingers trail the outside of my legs to the hem of my dress, his touch burning into my muscles. He continues his exploration, and with every inch he discovers, desire floods my core. I can feel my wetness run down the inside of my thighs. I attach one leg to his hip as soon as my lower half is fully exposed. His fingers splay over my cheek, biting my skin with his grip.

Without a word, George sinks to his knees and hooks my leg over his shoulder. *Dear God.*

"Well, if that isn't a pleasant surprise, Mania." He chuckles, the warmth of his breath the only warning before his tongue flicks against my clit, and I throw my head back. "Oh, fuck."

My reaction seems to be what he was hoping for. The hand not holding on to my ass begins to move. His nails rake over my flesh, dominating my nerve endings into a frenzy. When he reaches my core, he doesn't hesitate. Two fingers enter me with one thrust, and a loud moan erupts deep in my soul.

George continues to *taste* me, pumping in and out of my heat. My leg, still connected to the ground, begins to shake as I near a point of no return. He removes his mouth from my pussy, peering up at me. In the dim light, his obsidian eyes give him a menacing aura, which spurs my need for him even more. We live in a cruel world. George Weiler is one of the good ones, and I want to be his.

"Once I'm done eating, I'm going to fuck every guy that has or ever will touch you out of you." His statement mingles with the music drifting through the floor from downstairs. His tone is low, holding a vow neither of us has any power over.

George doesn't wait for me to reply before nipping on my sensitive spot. My teeth sink into my bottom lip as my eyes roll back. My fingers dive into his hair, curling inward and tugging. He growls and reciprocates by adding a third finger, stretching me.

"Shit, yes!"

His tongue assaults me until the pleasure becomes too much. Stars explode behind my lids, and I can't hold back, screaming his name. I ride out my orgasm, holding on to the kneeling man in front of me like my life depends on it.

George places gentle kisses on my inner thigh, followed by licking away my juices coating my skin.

Slowly rightening to his full height, he carefully dislodges my leg from his shoulder. He fists the material of my dress and pulls it up until it leaves me bared to him.

I can only watch as he shrugs out of his jacket and begins to unbutton his vest. Saliva pools in my mouth the more I get to see of him. I remember watching him run track in high school and spying with Car on all the male firstborns on the wrestling team from behind the bleachers. He was good-looking then. Drinking in his corded muscles now, he is truly a god—*my Ares.*

As he reaches for his pants, the cord connecting rationality to action snaps, and I swat his fingers away. I want to be the one to undress him. George lets his arms fall to his sides, his expression between a challenge and struggling to give up control. If he thinks I'll take my time, he's mistaken. I need him naked and inside me.

Pushing his pants down, they pool at his feet. My eyes are locked on his dick. The girth and length... He stands erect, taunting me to have my own taste. As much as I want to, I want to feel him fill me up even more.

George toes off his shoes and rids himself of his pants. With snakelike precision, his arm shoots out and wraps around my waist. He pulls me against him so fast I can only react. My palm touches the side of his face, and I hold his gaze.

"There is no turning back after this." My tone is low, and we both know what it means if we take the final step.

"You were mine from the moment I laid eyes on you at *Underworld*." He drops his forehead to mine.

I believe he means it, but *words* don't hold power in our world.

CHAPTER FIVE

GEORGE

LEAVING LOU THIS MORNING AND BOARDING THE JET FELT LIKE gutting myself with a blunt knife. Learning how to assassinate someone at 1700 yards was easier than saying goodbye to her while still draped in my sheets. I peer out of the small window, watching the seemingly unmoving clouds.

I replay last night over and over. I didn't mean for it to ever go this far—the consequences looming over our heads. Yet, when she stood in front of me in her dress, her blonde hair done in a perfect '20s do...she was a vision. Reason exited for the need to make her mine, no matter the repercussions. We could find a way. I would speak to my father—beg if I had to. Penny could take my position if it meant keeping Lou.

AFTER DECLARING SHE WAS MINE, Lou's eyes fluttered closed, and a pit in my stomach ripped open. What had I done? We both knew there was no future. But when her chocolate-colored irises gazed back at me, a new expression had overtaken her features—defiance mixed with desire.

Her hand slipped from my neck to my chest, and she shoved. Not expecting such force, I staggered. She bypassed me and aimed straight for my bed.

Placing her palms on the mattress, she peered over her shoulder. "Are you going to make good on your promise, Ares?" The way she gnawed on her bottom lip...a current of raw need zapped through me.

My hands were on her ass a few minutes ago, but now, with the curves of her perfect rear on display like that...my cock twitched with anticipation. My legs moved on autopilot. Stroking my dick slowly, methodically, I relished how she tracked every step.

The closer I got, the brighter the lust in her eyes shone. As soon as I was within reach, my fingers slid along her lower back. I'd never felt skin that soft. Chasing her spine to her neck, goose bumps erupted in my path. I wrapped my hand around her nape, squeezing lightly. I leaned forward, removing the last distance between us. Feverish heat hovered between our bodies, creating sparks ready to ignite.

My nose nuzzled her ear. "What's your kink, Mania? Tell me what you want."

Giving up *some* of my control elicited a hum in her throat. "I'm quite fond of sensory deprivation."

Well, fuck.

Images started to form in front of my mind's eye.

"I can work with that, babe." I nipped on her earlobe. "Don't move."

Who knew that Eloise Cartwright was a girl after my own heart? I still had the ties I had tried on earlier (and then forgone) draped over the bottom of my bed. Rolling my lips under, pondering this readily available prop and my intent for it, I grabbed one. Taking her first sense, I secured it behind her head in a double knot. Her breathing accelerated, and I stood back. Her excitement was mimicked in the erratic thundering behind my rib cage, yet I refused to show her what she did to me.

I brushed my fore- and middle finger from her tailbone, grazing playfully over her third hole and down to her aching heat. Easing a finger in with excruciating slowness, I studied Lou's reactions. Her head tilted up slightly, and her lips parted. I envisioned her rolling her eyes back.

"On the mattress."

As Lou followed my command, I withdrew and brought my fingers to my mouth. Sucking her from my skin, I murmured, "So sweet, Mania."

Lou positioned herself on all fours in the center of my king-size bed, and I reached over to my nightstand, grabbing my headphones and CD player.

"Lie on your back and put your arms over your head." My breathing picked up. She'd be at my mercy. The satisfaction mingled with the desire aching in my chest.

I grabbed another tie and bound her hands. "Your arms stay up here. Is that understood?"

Lou squirmed, rubbing her thighs together. "Yes."

The scent of her arousal filled the air. My teeth sank into my bottom lip as I watched her perky tits rise and fall. Her pebbled nipples begged for me to suck them into my mouth. *Soon.* My hand shot out and gripped her chin. Angling it in my direction, I leaned close. "Yes, what?" I licked the seam of her lips.

"Yes, Ares." Her reply ended in a moan, and my self-control tore like a frayed thread. I meshed my lips with hers, and it was my turn to groan.

I separated our mouths, and a protesting whimper filled the air. I chuckled. "So needy."

Placing the headphone cups over her ears, I pressed play. I

turned the volume of "Heart-Shaped Box" by Nirvana up until its muted sounds filled my room.

Her body tensed for a fraction of a second before she rendered herself into my down comforter.

"Mania." When she didn't react, the tips of my fingers tingled. The desire to touch her morphed from simmering to a burning compulsion. But I also needed to fuck her.

I moved between her legs, watching her pant with the unknown.

What would I do?

If we had the luxury of time, I wouldn't let this side of me out to play just yet. I would ease her in, worship her the way she deserved. But we had mere hours. Cupping her knees with my palms, I pushed her to open up. I stared at her glistening pussy —so ready.

Her hips bucked, and I tightened my hold.

Reaching around, my hands splayed on the backs of her thighs, and I guided her into position. I literally folded her in half with her knees by her ears and her ass and cunt on display for me to do as I pleased. She kept her arms over her head as I ordered her to.

Good girl.

Adjusting my restraint, I placed my forearm in the crook of her knee and gripped her other leg in the same spot. I raised my now free hand and let it crack on her cheek.

Where any other woman would've shrieked, Lou only sucked in a breath, followed by a moan. I wished she could hear me. I was impressed with how well she behaved and wanted to praise her for it.

Part of me longed to torture her with pleasure, bring her to the brink of insanity by depriving her of her orgasm. I wanted to give her a taste of what her future held by experiencing it herself —what her role in *The Order* would make her do to others to make them comply. But then again, we didn't have the time we should've had.

With her still immobile, I gripped my painfully hard length. I fisted my cock, pumping up and down once, twice, while watching the precum drip from the tip.

The overwhelming drive to feel her around me had me align with her opening. Lou twitched at the contact but then stilled. I watched her tits bounce as she panted with anticipation.

No longer able to contain myself, I sheathed myself to the hilt with one thrust. I groaned at the sensation of heat surrounding my dick, immediately clamping down. I couldn't order her not to come. She couldn't hear me. Sensing the unspoken command, Lou drew in a long, shaky breath and relaxed around me.

I dropped my arm from her legs, allowing her to place them on either side. I let my body fall forward, caging her between my arms as I began moving. With every thrust, I struggled to regain control over the havoc racking me. Emotions I had never experienced mingled with primal lust, short-circuiting my brain.

Pumping in and out of her tight pussy, I fused my lips to her nipple, sucking it into my mouth. I propped myself on one side, palming her free breast with the other. I rolled her hard nipple between my teeth before gently biting down—enough to cause a sting but not draw blood.

"Oh, fuck. Yes." Her words were breathless.

Her ecstasy sent every nerve ending into overdrive. She rolled her hips in sync with my thrusts, both of us speeding up as my dick thickened inside her.

Letting go of her breast, I captured her lips. My fingers threaded into her hair, which had come undone as I ground her into my pillows. Curling the strands around my fists, I tugged. Not once did Lou drop her arms, and had she been able to see, she would've caught my approval. Our kisses turned frantic, no doubt leaving marks for everyone to notice by morning. I didn't care, though. Being with Lou was worth the wrath of the devil.

I felt her walls clamp around my cock at the same time my balls tightened. Not taking my eyes off the woman underneath me as I rode out waves of the best orgasm I had ever experienced, a new sensation exploded inside my chest.

I was so screwed.

CHAPTER SIX

GEORGE

IT'S BEEN FIVE MONTHS SINCE I HELD LOU.

In one week, I have to report to my unit, and I have no
fucking clue when I will see her next. A sharp pain shoots
through my skull, my jaw having been locked since boarding the
plane. What am I going to walk into? Paper crinkles between my
fingers, and I peer down at her last letter.

My Ares,

*Next week is my 22nd birthday. I don't think I ever told you the
exact date, did I? But even if...you probably know. I wish you could be
here. Mother planned this elaborate party at the Altman. I mean, really?
They're probably using my party for some business play against the old
man. I'd take The Carlyle or even Underworld over this stuck-up hotel.
Did I say that I wish you could be there?*

I DON'T FINISH READING. I've pretty much memorized it.

THE MEMORY of how Lou scribbled the address to a post office box with tears in her eyes pushes to the forefront. She was still draped in my sheet, the party long over. Neither of us had left the room after we...

She wrote every week, and I returned her words as often as I could. We avoided the topic that would eventually catch up to us: time. My heartbeat slows to a painful rhythm. In two years, Davis and I would take our places as two of the three leaders in *The Order*.

I STEP out of the town car, staring at the golden *A* adorning the massive wrought iron doors. I had asked Penny to deliver my tux to the hangar and changed on the jet.

My mouth runs dry as I take my first step, and I pause. Everyone will be in there. How will Lou react? I can't greet her the way I want. All eyes will be on her.

I curl and flex my fingers. Approaching the entrance, the muscles in my back coil. I may have been gone, but *The Order's* guards that replaced the usual bellhops don't question my attendance. They hold the massive doors open, avoiding direct eye contact.

NO ONE PAYS me any attention when I enter the grand ballroom. I heard that Altman replicated the original hotel from Los Angeles with this one. Not a cheap undertaking, given the footprint here goes up instead of out.

A champagne fountain the size of a small high-rise takes over the center. Round tables, fitting over a dozen people each, are positioned circularly around the room. I scan the crowd, spotting my parents talking to Davis's old man and Mr. Altman to my right—I go left.

Slowly making my way along the outskirts of the setup, I finally see her. Lou stands underneath one of the massive crystal chandeliers, and my heart squeezes. She looks breathtaking. Her blonde hair frames her face in loose curls. She is draped in a white gown, accentuating every curve. My fingers twitch to run my hands up and down her body. Fiery heat spreads through every cell, my pants becoming uncomfortably tight. The material of her dress glows under the illumination, making a golden aura appear around her. Car and Nic flank Lou, scanning the group of randoms pretty much worshiping her with disdain.

"I was wondering if you would make it," a low voice states near my ear.

The warmth I felt a moment ago turns to ice. I don't face him. "Wouldn't miss it for the world."

Davis steps to my side. "You have no future." His words hold an undertone like he is not just talking about Lou.

Ignoring how my pulse thunders through my veins, I imagine it crushing the ice my best friend injected into shards. Inhaling slowly, I inquire as if none of this bothers me, "And you do?"

"*The Order* sets the rules, G." His monotone statement ignites the rage I've contained since falling for Eloise Cartwright. I whirl around and push Davis against the wall, my forearm against his throat. The pounding in my ears drowns out the constant stream of meaningless chatter hanging in the air. He doesn't flinch. Despite the pressure, his breathing remains even. *Pain is not real.* One of the first lessons we learn when we begin our training.

A hand lands on my arm. Davis tilts his head and glances to my side. My head slowly swivels in the same direction, and my eyes connect with a pair of dark-brown irises.

Everything is right again.

I drop my hold, and my best friend smirks. He lifts his hand, saluting Lou with his tumbler. "Happy birthday, Eloise." He sidesteps me, but before he passes Lou, he bends down and kisses her on the cheek. He whispers something in her ear, and she stiffens. Lou gives Davis a curt nod without ever taking her eyes off me.

Finally alone, I cup her elbow and lead her to one of the side doors.

In the dim light of the abandoned hallway, I turn her to face me. "What did he want?" My question is harsh, but the tension in my body has reached its snapping point.

Lou touches her gloved hand to my cheek. "You're here."

Hearing her words instantly calms my buzzing nerves. I frame her face with my palms and press my mouth to hers. "My Mania."

Lou moans, swiping her tongue over my lips. "Ares."

This is all I need to hear. She is still mine. I crowd her backward until her back hits the wall, and my hands find her hips. My fingers dig into the fabric of her gown—a white gown, as I notice while kissing my way down the column of her throat.

"I missed you," I confess. I kept my letters to her neutral, fearing someone could find them and punish her.

"Not as much as I missed you." Her small fingers fist my tux shirt. Her tongue tangles with mine in a ravishing dance for who needs the other more. We can't hide here all night. Lou would be missed soon—

"Eloise!" A whisper-shout makes us recoil from each other. "Your mother is looking for you."

Carolyn stares at us with a sneer. She may be one of Lou's best friends, but I don't trust her. Where Lou is Mania, and I'm Ares, Carolyn is Echidna. Instead of being Typhon's mate, though, she pursued the devil and stabbed everyone in the back —laughing—to reach her goal.

Lou searches my eyes, the hesitation coming off her in waves. One touch was not nearly enough.

"I'm not leaving," I assure her. "Go celebrate your birthday, and I'll find you later."

CHAPTER SEVEN

LOU

WHILE I PRETENDED TO ENJOY MY PARTY, GEORGE RENTED A room at the Altman. The evening was one of my best charades to this day.

I smiled at my guests as they approached me to gush about the gown my mother forced on me and congratulate me as if twenty-two was some special number. By the end of the night, I felt like my cheeks would permanently be suspended in this Joker-like grimace. The dress was beautiful. Putting it on, I immediately pictured walking down the aisle in it—with George waiting for me. But here...it made me look like a misplaced bride. The soft fabric was suffocating, making it harder to bring oxygen to my lungs the longer the night went on. What kind of game was Mother playing? The contracts had been set in stone since I was in diapers. It wasn't like I had to prove anything to anyone, yet maybe she had to. Who knew what was going on in the rankings of *The Order*?

As it all came to a close, I informed my parents that Nic had invited me to stay with her for the next few days. Her parents were out of town. We had planned my escape since the day Mother announced this farce. Nic was my only friend who was not part of this unhinged lifestyle. My parents didn't associate with *Norms*. I didn't have to worry about them checking on my whereabouts when I was with her.

I'll make it up to her later.

Confirming Car was busy with Marshall, I chased Nic to the washroom.

"You need to cover for me." My words came in spurts, caused by racing after her and the gown restricting my airways. I steadied myself against the wall, blocking the door with my body. I didn't need anyone to walk in on us. Sweat trickled down the nape of my neck.

Nic was washing her hands, her eyes flying to mine in the mirror. Her eyes narrowed, scanning me up and down as if it would provide her the answer to her unspoken question.

She may not have grown up with us, but she'd picked up on things over the last year. Marshall didn't make a secret about who we were or what we did—no one betrayed *The Order*.

She cocked her head. "Are you okay?"

At her question, my internal temperature spiked even more. Biting the inside of my cheek, I wanted to answer her honestly. *No.* Instead, I drew my shoulders back and swallowed the needles pricking the back of my throat. "Of course. I just need to...do something for a few days."

Vague much?

Nic gnawed on her cheek for a moment before nodding. "Okay."

GEORGE and I spent three days in our tiny sanctuary. Draped between the sheets, we talked for hours. He indulged me with reruns of my favorite childhood TV show, and, of course, he played into every fantasy I envisioned with him over the last few months.

Penny dropped off his duffel with clothes on day two. He assured me that we could trust his sister, and when he pulled out his ties and CD player, my palms covered my flaming cheeks. It was perfect. *He* was perfect.

Yet, he would never be mine.

The thought hit me randomly while George took a shower. My shoulders curled forward, and a void overtook my body. The happiness and...*love* I felt since spotting him in the ballroom got sucked out of me, and I burst into tears. There was nothing left. I should have felt empty, yet the space in my chest felt too tight. Nothing made sense. I watched my tears drop to the sheet covering my lap, staining the shiny cream fabric. I pulled my knees up and curled into the tiniest ball I could manage. Maybe if I pressed close enough, something would fill the gaping hole that made my ribs ache. What was going on with me? Did *Mania* already consume me?

In my hysteria, I didn't hear George exit the bathroom. Arms suddenly wound around me. His wet chest registered against my naked back, and droplets fell from his hair to my shoulder. I shivered at the contrast between our mingling body heat and the coolness of the water.

"I'm here, baby. We'll figure this out. I promise." His murmured assurances eased some of the despair.

Would we, though? Figure it out?

AGREEING that we shouldn't be seen together, George left twenty minutes ago. I spent extra time refolding my unworn clothes into my Louis Vuitton Keepall. It had sat unused in the corner of the room since I dropped it there.

When it's my time to go, I watch the numbers descend on the digital display of the elevator, going over everything I have scheduled for the rest of the week and when I could sneak away for a few hours.

The doors glide open, and my heart stutters in my chest before taking off in a sprint. I'm face to face with Car. She seems equally surprised. Her brows arch in a perfect, plucked semicircle before they dip into a frown. She takes a step back, letting me exit the elevator. My fingers tighten around the handles of my bag.

"I thought you were with Nic." Her narrowed eyes glitter with mistrust.

"I—" *I have no idea what to say.*

"Did he ask you to come here, too?" Car's tone turns to ice.

Huh?

Like George and Marshall, we've been best friends by association since we were kids, born into the same world and raised under the same rules. But it becomes clear as she levels me that I was never *her friend*.

"I don't know what you—" I blink.

People approach, pressing the button to call one of the elevators, and Car latches on to my wrist. She drags me around the corner to where the ice machine is hidden from view.

Her nails dig into my skin, and I rip away. "What the fuck? Let go of me."

Facing off with her in the small alcove, she lets her true colors appear like a shiny aura. Car curls her lips. "When were you supposed to meet him? I still have two years before he is—" She stops herself abruptly, poking my chest with her purple manicured nail. "Leave us—"

I shove her shoulder with my free hand, and she stumbles against the wall with an oomph sound. "Do not touch me, you crazy bitch." We're nose to nose, and I smell the booze on her breath. "What the fuck is going on with you?" I put distance between us, not wanting to cause a scene.

Unfortunately, my friend doesn't have the same reasoning. She follows me, slanting her head. "He's mine." The stench of stale wine fills my nose, and I swallow over the sour taste it elicits in my throat. "I don't care what the council says. I will—"

"Carolyn."

My spine stiffens, and Car presses her lips in a thin line, swallowing her next words. We pivot toward the large figure hovering in the opening of our hiding spot.

Marshall wears his trademark jeans and tee, a cigarette hanging from the corner of his lips. His eyes are cold, the opposite of George's—their friendship probably forced on them, like mine with Car.

Car opens her mouth but snaps it shut when Marshall's hand wraps itself around her throat. He drags her close until his lips hover near hers, the cherry of his cigarette almost touching her face. I have no doubt she feels the heat, but Car doesn't flinch. A faint blush slithers up her neck, and she actually whimpers—relishing the devil's attention, no matter how deranged it is.

"Go upstairs and wait for me, Carolyn." There is no cadence in Marshall's command.

He lets go of her and tips her chin up with his thumb and forefinger. No additional words cross his lips. He lets the power radiating off his body speak for itself.

Suddenly, my friend's gaze shifts. Equal disdain overtakes her features. She tears her face away from Marshall's and throws me a loathing glance before stalking back toward the elevator bank.

I hold Marshall's amused—at the same time, non-comical—gaze until we hear the ding of my friend's departure. He crosses his arms over his chest, resembling George in build and muscle mass, but that's where the similarities end.

"Did you have fun, Eloise?" The way he emphasizes my full name makes my mouth run dry.

"Why do you care?" I blink away the dizziness his nearness causes. I refuse to let him treat me like every other female. He may be in charge soon, but as of now, we are of the same rank.

He contemplates my question, his eyes raking over my body.

The skin over my knuckles burns from tension as I still grip the bag.

Marshall takes a step closer. He's not crowding me but making sure I have to tilt my head up to meet his eyes. I swallow over the choking noise trying to escape my lips.

"I don't care." He retreats until he is back in the hallway. "But you should if you want to survive what's to come."

He swivels smoothly on his heels and disappears from sight.

My lips part as my body is consumed with terror. Marshall Davis is planning something.

CHAPTER EIGHT

LOU

ONE YEAR LATER

HE'S DEPLOYING. My eyes read the message. It registers in my brain. Yet, I'm looking at a word puzzle. Random letters make up sentences—a message I never wanted to receive.

My palm presses to my chest in a failed attempt to force oxygen to reach my lungs. I can't breathe. I'm sitting in my usual booth at *The Daily Brew*, a.k.a. TDB—a café down the street from the post office. I've become a regular here since I wrote down the address to my PO box for George after our first night together. I've come here with every new letter, needing the privacy of a busy New York café to read the words connecting me to the man I love.

A sour taste coats my tongue as images of George injured—or worse—play in my mind like my grandparents' eight-millimeter projector. Black spots fade in and out, the nightmarish visions blending with people leaving and entering through the revolving door. A crinkling sound reaches my ears, forcing the images away. My focus shifts, and— No, no, no. I drop the letter. My fingers had clutched it to the point of tearing. It floats to the tabletop, and I frantically smooth it back out. Tears cloud my sight as I stare at the small rip in the middle of his words. What if this is the last letter I will ever receive, and I ruined it? I bite my cheek until a metallic taste fills my mouth.

"You okay, Lou?" Tina, one of the waitresses, stops by my side.

I swipe at my eyes, probably causing more harm to my makeup than good. "Yes." I flip the letter over. "I'm fine. Just got some unexpected news." I pull the corners of my mouth up.

She follows my movement. When her hand lands on my shoulder, I involuntarily flinch, and she recoils quickly. "Well, uh...okay. Shout if you need anything."

Tina doesn't buy my explanation, but I don't care. I don't trust anyone these days. I nod and mumble a thank-you.

She studies me for another moment before finally walking to the next customer.

Tension melts from my muscles as my gaze drops to the letter. Splaying my fingers over it, I focus on the sensation of it against my palm.

When I rented the PO box, its purpose was to be able to receive mail I didn't want our maid to report back to my parents. As a teenager with a fake ID, being able to subscribe to magazines let me pretend to be normal, seeming like a huge achievement. In my twenties, this frivolous accomplishment allowed me to exchange letters with the man I loved with all my soul.

Finally, the cramping sensation behind my ribs eases, and I inhale a wheezing breath.

For the past twelve months, George has been three thousand miles across the country while I've remained in my family's home in New York. After our run-in at the Altman, Car refused to talk to me. And with Nic still deep-throating Marshall's dick... well, I choose to stay away from her as well.

The only time I commute outside of the city is when I report to the Institute. My presence there has been requested more frequently. The reason...something I'm not proud of: I am good at my job. My education, combined with the skills that—*according to Mother*—run in our blood, allows me to get quicker results than any of my parents' medical staff holding multiple PhDs.

I spend two more hours at TDB. The streetlights have come on by the time I finally slide out of the booth. I have six weeks before he is halfway across the world and I may never see him again.

DESPERATION DROVE me to try any phone number I could dig up for George's base, which, given my limitation to the public phone directory, resulted in a whoppin' three calls—all ending in...nothing.

The first asshole hung up on me. The second at least let me get my name and reason for calling out before he informed me in a curt tone that he was unable to help. The last one suggested sending another letter.

At his words, my throat closed up, and I dropped the receiver. Sure, I could write a letter, but what good would it do? George was on the other side of the country, and I had no way or reason to travel to the West Coast. Mother would never allow it. Even if she did, what was I going to do? Throw a fit at the gate? I felt like a modern-day Juliet trapped in a world of...*The Order*. One of us would die—if not both. Stifling the sobs burning like acid in my chest, I covered my mouth. The last thing I needed was to alert anyone in the house. I cried until my insides felt hollow. I clung to the shred of hope not yet disintegrated, but I could already feel the ember dying in my core.

Over the next week and a half, I wrote six letters. They all ended with the same words.

I love you. Please come back to me.

I BARELY LEFT my house during that time and missed four sessions at the Institute. When I reported for my next shift, I didn't make it past the foyer. Father appeared at the top of the stairs, his arms behind his back. I scanned his impassive expression, and a sensation of icy tendrils choked me, constricting my ability to breathe.

A voice in the back of my head screamed to run. I knew that look. Without breaking the visual connection, I took one step backward but got stopped by a wall. No, not a wall. A body. I whirled around, but before I made it the whole hundred and eighty degrees, something sharp punctured my arm. Another person had approached from the side and was now holding an empty syringe.

Mother?

Cold sweat began to coat my skin, and my stomach rolled. The guard that had stopped my attempt to flee peered down at me with a sneer. His face blurred, and I forced the nausea back down. I would not hurl. They couldn't do that to... I needed—

My knees gave out.

I'M GOING to be sick. What the—

A groan escapes my lips, and I bite my tongue. Do not make

a sound. *Where am I?* My chest aches as my heart begins to thunder against my ribs. I blink, but... *Why can't I see?*

I touch my palm to my forehead. My clothes stick to my body, and unease crawls up my spine. My fingers carefully explore my surroundings. The icy sting of tiles hits me like a sledgehammer. *No!* They wouldn't do that.

A rustle on the other side of my confinement makes my muscles freeze. I squeeze my lids shut, fighting against the sensation of vertigo. Holding my breath, I wait. I'm not alone. Time stands still. When my lungs begin to burn, I force shallow breaths to supply my body with what it demands.

A crackling sound comes over the intercom before he speaks. "You disappoint me, Eloise." My father's reprimand is confirmation that I have become the lesson.

I want to scream that I only missed four sessions. They have enough fucking personnel to reform their *patients* three times over. But the point isn't that I inconvenienced the Institute. It's about defying him.

I lock my jaw. There's no point in arguing. I know how this place operates. The more you fight, the harder they come down on you—the more painful the exercise. "Yes, Father."

More crackling.

"This is your chance to fix your mistake."

Oh, shit.

I jackknife into a sitting position before shifting to a crouch. I distribute my weight between the balls of my feet, one hand propping me up. My free hand rests by my side, ready to snap forward at anyone coming at me. The surge in adrenaline overshadows my body's violent desire to purge itself of anything remaining in my stomach.

"Joshua is currently restrained across from you. Since you delayed his reformation, it is your responsibility to deal with the consequences. We stopped his *medication*."

He cannot be serious. JT has been a *Tester*. Old Man Davis introduced the *Taste Testers*—as he calls them—after someone laced his merch with poison a few years back. Now, nothing gets distributed without being sampled first. Unfortunately for this particular guy, he got a little too addicted to his job. High as a kite, he tried to steal five hundred grams of coke—with his boss in the room. Moron.

Now, his options are withdrawal and start over or...ending his employment permanently. If they stopped weaning him, he would be more dangerous than some of our enforcers in his current state.

"What do you want me to do in here without meds for him?" I grit out. And why hasn't JT made a sound yet?

A soft chuckle reaches my ears through the speaker. "He is past the point of rehabilitation."

Fucking hell. They want me to put him down.

"We left you a few tools to up the stakes a little bit. Don't let me down again, Eloise."

CHAPTER NINE

GEORGE

MY FINGERS TOUCH HER LETTERS IN MY PASSENGER SEAT. Sitting in my grandfather's '72 GTO, I haven't taken my eyes off the high-rise where Lou's parents have their condo in the city. Their main residence is outside of New York, near the Institute, for convenience.

I arrived thirty-six hours ago. After Penny informed me that no one had seen Lou in over a week, I jumped on the first commercial flight. Thankfully, my leave was already approved by my CO. Otherwise, the timing would've sucked—and most likely caused me a dishonorable discharge.

In one of her first letters this last year, Lou wrote that she had distanced herself from pretty much everyone—a gesture that equally relieved me as it scared me. There was no such thing as leaving *The Order*. Alive.

Before I reported to my unit, I asked Penny to befriend Lou. While Lou never mentioned it to me, Penny was able to lure my girlfriend out for coffee every few weeks. *Girlfriend.* She couldn't be, but she was. And yet the term wasn't nearly enough. The knowledge of one person in my corner eased the constant restlessness. I spoke to my parents regularly, usually business related, but it allowed me to get an update from my sister.

However, my last call made me feel like getting suffocated by a pillow. As soon as Penny's words registered, my lungs stopped functioning. I inhaled—or tried to. No air would reach its target.

"I called the condo. The housekeeper said Lou was supposed to be back a week ago, but her parents informed her that she would be staying at the mansion for a few more days. G, Lou hates it there. We both know that." Penny's recollection had ended on a pitch. She was scared—for Lou. My insides felt like Penny was tearing them to shreds with her words. With every syllable, a new stabbing sensation punctured my heart. I bent over, resting my forehead against my knees in an attempt to regain some control.

"I want you over there. Talk to the housekeeper. Find out where Lou really is," I demanded, my voice muffled against my cammies. There was no way the staff didn't know. The Cartwrights were as unhinged as the rest—maybe even worse, given their specialty. They didn't bother hiding shit. If anyone dared talk, he or she would find themselves in one of the Institute's cells faster than a human anchor sinks in the Hudson. Straightening, I finally managed a breath. "I'll call you back from the airport."

PENNY DIDN'T FIND out much. However, the housekeeper let it slip (by accident or on purpose) that Lou was expected back the next day. She was tasked with cleaning up and preparing meals for her.

And here I am. I borrowed my grandfather's beloved car from the storage unit and stalked Lou's city residence. The only time I left my post was to grab food and take a piss. And Penny took my spot during those eight-minute sprints down the block.

I'm about to reach for Lou's last letter—rereading her words slowed my racing pulse every time—when a blacked-out SUV passes me. Instead of stopping at the front entrance, it pulls into the alley next to the building. My gaze drops to the license plate, and adrenaline vibrates through every nerve ending. On autopilot, I reach under the seat, removing the .44 Mag my grandfather keeps in here. While many vehicles like this exist, especially in New York, *The Order* has very distinct license plates—a subtle way to recognize the family and driver. Given my role and position, I made it my goal to learn everyone's mode of transportation.

I slide out of the GTO. Where Lou's absence had caused me a near panic attack, I am in my element now. My pulse is as calm and steady as if I were asleep. Training has taken over my body, my brain handling the situation how I was taught when entering enemy territory. Enemies—that's what they had become.

I approach the mouth of the alley in time to see the back door open. Her leg is the first thing I notice. But what registers next spurs my steady heartbeat to a thundering sprint. Her pant leg is torn. Hanging in threads. Lou braces herself with her palm against the door as if exiting the SUV causes her physical pain. A red haze invades my vision, and everything I was taught is forgotten. My girlfriend is hurt. My feet start moving. With every step, I pick up speed. While physically getting closer, my tunnel vision makes it appear as if I barely move.

Lou's head swivels in my direction, and her lips part. She pales. Scanning her surroundings, her eyes dart around. Bile rises in my throat when her full appearance registers in my brain. Her blonde hair is caked with...blood. I swallow over the vile taste rising from the pit of my stomach. I refuse to let emotions take control. I need to get to her. Touch her. Make sure she is safe.

The more my brain catalogs, the faster my pulse thrashes. Her lower lip is split, and bruises shadow her usually smooth skin. My fingers tighten around the grip of my revolver.

I will kill whoever did this.

She leans into the car, speaking to someone, yet never losing sight of me. I slow my strides, giving her time to do whatever she — Straightening, she slams the door shut, and the SUV begins to move. Pretending I'm not there, Lou pivots toward the back entrance and inserts her key. She pulls on the handle and disappears into the high-rise without a backward glance.

My steps slow to a walk. Before the door closes on me, my arm shoots out. My hand blocks me from being locked out, and I slip through the narrow gap.

The industrial lights blind me, and I blink. Adjusting to the glare, Lou comes into view. The emotional overload ranges from relief to concern to the most feral rage I've ever experienced.

Heart hammering in my chest, we stand across from each other. I tuck the revolver in the back of my jeans. Lou holds my gaze, and her eyes gloss over. When her bottom lip begins to tremble, I can no longer remain in place. Taking one step in her direction, she flies into my arms. I crush her to me. The ability to hold her, feel her, is not nearly enough. Lou clings to my midsection, her shoulders shaking as sobs rack through her thin frame. She's lost weight.

"Y-you—here." Her muffled cries break me.

I disentangle myself enough to look at her. In this light, I see that the bruises marring her beautiful face are not as fresh as I initially thought. I frame her cheeks, carefully leaning my forehead to hers. Her chocolate-brown irises are muddled with tears, and she peers at me through her lashes.

"What happened, Mania?"

CHAPTER TEN

LOU

I INHALE HIS EXHALE, THE SCENT OF COFFEE SETTLING ON MY tongue. My fists clutch the front of his shirt, afraid that if I let go, I will find myself back in the room at the Institute.

"Baby, if you don't start talking, I will tear this town apart to get answers. And I'll begin with the Cartwright house of horrors."

Razor blades slice the back of my throat. Pain from days of deprivation. I lost track of how long I was gone. What I do remember is the number of cups of water I received while I was locked in with—*Don't think about him.* Ten.

"I paid the price," I whisper, not because I don't want him to hear me or because I'm scared, but because I lost the ability to use my voice. I screamed until there was nothing left, until I was an empty shell trapped in the four walls of my reformation chamber—Joshua's chamber.

George's nostrils flare as his lips curl back. A snarl reverberates through the bare hallway, but I'm not sure he's even aware of the noise coming from him. For the first time, he resembles the person he is supposed to become: one of *the three*. Marshall Davis has nothing on him at this moment. Rage emanates from him in waves, and I have no doubt he would kill anyone in his path for answers.

Despite my body's protests, I untangle myself from him. George makes me feel safe. He would never hurt me. But we can't have this conversation here. Father ordered our driver not to let me go through the main entrance—looking like the victim of a violent crime would cause too many questions. Little would anyone suspect, I wasn't the victim in this scenario. I was the executioner.

Interlacing our fingers, I lead George through the maze I call home. He walks beside me with determined strides, his eyes sweeping our surroundings, prepared for anything. His callused pads feel rough against my palm, a sensation others would declare unpleasant. Yet the connection sends tingles to parts of my body that should not be interested in anything but a shower and clean clothes.

My parents own the entire thirty-second floor. We have a private elevator situated away from the *Norms*. It's unlikely we'll run into anyone. Plus, I don't expect anyone to be there. Our maid leaves by five. Even if she is there, she'd never betray me. She's the one person my parents employ that I trust.

I watch the numbers on the display ascend. Thirty, thirty-one, thirty-two. The doors glide open, and George's hand tightens around mine. His shoulders are pulled back, and he has the Mag back in his grip.

"No one is here." My raspy voice cracks at the last word.

His posture doesn't change. He positions himself partially in front of me as I enter the foyer. His protectiveness thaws the void that had taken over every cell.

My parents believe I was reeducated. They didn't calculate George into the equation. If he hadn't shown up, I might have let the *lesson* consume me—another step closer to fate and my future chiseled in the marble walls of the Institute. But he's here.

I lead us to my bedroom, our quiet footfalls *echoing* off the bare walls. My mother designed the condo as an extension of my parents' place of work—what they consider their real home.

Crossing the threshold, I halt in my tracks. My gaze swipes over my king-size bed with its black-and-red skull-pattern pillows and duvet. During my junior year in high school, I painted my walls burgundy after Mother once again complained about my insolent behavior during one of *The Order's* events. None of this was me, yet it was the only physical place I felt at peace. It represented everything I didn't want to be—the destiny looming over my head.

My sheets are unmade as of the day I left. My stomach knots and I involuntarily press my palm against my abdomen. George immediately closes the door and flips the lock. Not that this would stop anyone, but the gesture adds another layer of security to his presence.

He pivots me by our joined fingers until I face him. "Start talking, Mania."

I peer down at myself, something I have refused to do since fixing my mistake. The smell of blood and the dried substances from being locked in the chamber with his decomposing body no longer register. All I see is torn and stained fabric. I can only imagine how I must smell to George.

I shake my head and his lips part. I hold up a hand. "Shower first."

George's chest rises and falls in an attempt to rein in his urge for vengeance. He wants answers. Images of JT advancing on me fill my mind, and my chest tightens. I rise to my tiptoes, pressing my mouth carefully to his. It's been so long since I've seen him.

Felt him. I tease him with my tongue, and he opens up with a groan. A current surges through me, and all my guilt and resignation about who I am—supposed to be—gets swept away by a tidal wave of love, desire, and...hope.

George nips at my bottom lip, and lust becomes the dominant emotion. My hands reach for him of their own volition, unbuckling his belt frantically. I vaguely notice George placing the revolver on the dresser beside the door. He grasps the remnants of my shirt and pulls it over my head. Standing in front of him in my bra, I hold my breath, waiting for him to lose his shit. My entire side still aches, and I can imagine how the green and yellow bruises surround several healing cuts.

When he doesn't react, I dare meet his eyes. Blazing with heat and fury, he's battling for control. The muscle in his jaw tics, and I bite the inside of my cheek.

"Who did this?" George's tone promises revenge.

Cold sweat begins to coat my palms, and I stare at his obsidian irises, unblinking. "He's dead."

What if George sees me differently after he finds out...

A groove appears between his brows, forcing me to elaborate. "I killed him."

George's brows pop, and he levels me. "I hope you made him suffer."

A shaky laugh bubbles up in my dry throat as relief crashes through me. Instead of reliving the night I chose to survive, I begin walking backward, pulling the man I love more than my soul with me to the adjacent bathroom.

GEORGE MADE me forget the last eleven days. Eleven fucking days, as I found out when I finally told him everything later that night.

He slowly undressed the rest of me and turned on the shower while I stared at my reflection in the mirror. The eyes peering back at me were mine, but at the same time, they weren't. Not anymore. Steam slowly filled the room. I trailed the fading bruises and healing cuts, fighting a wince at the sight of the evidence JT left on my body. I knew they were there since I felt the sharp pain as he sliced me with the bowie knife. My only interaction while in the chamber was getting my injuries examined and cleaned. Once determined that I would survive and didn't need stitches, I was left alone until the door swung open to grant me my release.

The scars would give everyone enough material to gossip about for years.

George's arms wound around me from behind, and our gazes met. Some of his menace had tempered. "The only thing these marks say about you is that you are a survivor."

His words hit something deep in my core, and I meshed my lips under to prevent them from trembling. He took a step back and swiveled me around by the shoulders.

We stared at each other for twenty-seven breaths before he grasped my wrists and started walking backward, pulling me into the large walk-in shower. When the hot stream hit my skin, I groaned. I relished the sensation of everything washing away. I followed the stream of water as it disappeared down the drain. My tense muscles slowly loosened. Looking up, I noticed how the hot spray soaked George's remaining clothes, and my mouth ran dry. The material clung to his ripped muscles. He was toned before, but the last year had turned him into a machine.

Leaning against the tiled wall, I watched him rid himself of the last barriers between us.

He reached for the loofah and slathered it with my body wash. My stomach flipped in anticipation as the scent of vanilla filled the air. Cleaning me with a gentleness I'd never experienced before, my body drowned in the sensory stimulation. George kissed his way from my neck down to every mark my fight had left me with. Sinking to his knees, his large palms settled on my thighs. Holding my breath, I watched him study me through wet lashes.

"You are the most beautiful woman I've ever seen." I wanted to laugh his compliment off because, right now, I looked anything but beautiful. Then he flicked his tongue against my clit, and my brain short-circuited.

Over the next hours, George took care of me in more ways than I could ever repay him. He cleaned my skin, healed my soul, and worshiped my body in ways I never imagined. He was gentle at first, but when I sank to my knees under the scorching spray, wanting to reciprocate, all restraint left him. He grasped my arms and pulled me to my feet. Lifting me up by the ass, he slammed me against the wall. With my mind focused on other parts of my body, the expected pain didn't come. *Pain is not real.* He sheathed himself to the hilt, and everything fell away. I moaned as he drove into me with relentless need. A need I felt in every nerve ending. There was nothing I wouldn't let this man do to me tonight.

THE HORIZON SURROUNDING the buildings outside my window is already showing the first signs of morning when I lie with George's arms draped around me in my bed. The soft comforter feels like heaven on my naked skin after not having had anything to cover up with for so long.

George swipes a strand of hair from my face. "You managed to distract me there for a while, Mania." A crooked smile makes him appear boyish for a fraction of a second, then he amends, "Now it's time for you to talk." His tone is soft, yet the command behind his words is clear. His nose nudges mine in a caress.

The warm cocoon my duvet and his embrace have created becomes too tight. JT's voice fills my ears. The vile names he threw at me when the lights turned on and he realized I wasn't there to help him. The snarl he lunged at me with. My pulse spikes. Nausea rises in my throat, and I swallow. I'm safe. I'm with the man I love.

But for how long?

"After your letter"—heaviness weighs me down, remembering the day—"I missed several sessions." George's form blurs. "I was working with one of the testers, so he didn't have to be put down."

George studies me with an impassive expression. He knows how it works. The normality of how casually we speak about a life disgusts me. Yet, this is our world. I may still have a shred of humanity left, but I was raised in a society where people are commodities. If they no longer serve a purpose, we get rid of them.

"When I reported for my next shift..." My stomach knots, and I feel the phantom pain where my mother tranqed me. "My father"—why I leave *her* out of this, I have no clue—"made an example out of my disobedience."

George's eyes narrow, and he goes eerily still.

I draw in a long breath. "They put me in the chamber with JT."

"Joshua Taylor?" he interrupts, and I nod. Of course George knows the testers. Plus, JT has worked for Walter Davis since he plucked him off the streets as a teenager.

I press my lips together, which serves as his confirmation.

"My father told me to fix him. He'd been in withdrawal for days at this point. JT was completely delusional."

Understanding settles in the depths of his eyes. His lips part, but I shake my head. I need to get it off my chest, tell someone, even if it's just the CliffsNotes.

"At first, JT thought I was there to help him. You can't imagine the look of betrayal when he realized that—" My voice cracks.

George swipes the loose tear away with his thumb but remains mute.

"The room was dark. They had him gagged and restrained against the wall." Which explained why he didn't make much sound at first. "I knew I wasn't alone, but I couldn't see who was with me. When Father announced I was there to fix my mistake..." I hollow my cheeks.

"I asked what they wanted me to do without anything I usually use for the process." My heart thunders and it hurts to speak the words. "The overhead lights came on." Closing my lids, I attempt to block out the image that materializes. "They had left a whole arsenal in the middle of the floor. Knives, rope, a Taser, even a bamboo staff." My stomach bottoms out the same way as that day when the realization hit. *It was him or me.*

"The shackles released, and JT just stared. His eyes were bloodshot and—"

George brings his mouth to mine. The slight pressure against my lips unties all the knots my words have twisted inside me. "You are safe now. Nothing will ever happen to you again." He speaks the words without breaking the connection, and I want to believe him so badly.

We kiss for what feels like forever, but our impending futures loom over us. Eventually, George separates our lips and levels me with an expression that sends chills down my spine.

"I will speak to my father. He and Lee can overrule the contract." His hands frame my face, and my gaze ping-pongs between his eyes.

"They will never go for it. Marshall—"

"Will not lay a hand on you." The tips of his fingers apply pressure against my skull. "You are mine, Eloise Cartwright. My Mania. I am not going to give you up for a business deal. If my father and Lee don't cancel out the verdict, we'll run."

Hope floods my veins for the first time in years. George is serious. Together, we can fight fate.

CHAPTER ELEVEN

GEORGE

Thirteen months later

I STAND HIDDEN in the shadows. My fingers grip my grandfather's revolver to the point of my knuckles being on fire. Invisible to the world, I blend into the entrance of a closed shop across from the Altman and watch a scene unfold that cuts me open all over again.

Guards have replaced the hotel's staff. Tonight, *The Order* as we know it will come to an end, and *The Davis Order* will commence.

Black SUV after black SUV pulls up in front of the main entrance. The Cartwrights arrived a few minutes ago. Watching Mrs. Cartwright strut through the doors like she owned the place made me want to shoot her point blank. After Lou's parents come the Veils. Carolyn looks like the evil queen she aspires to be, draped in a floor-length black gown. However, loathing is written all over her face. She hates this as much as I do.

Penny is next, and my chest constricts. I only saw her three days ago when she met me at the airport. She handed me the meager belongings she was able to save. A knot forms in my stomach, remembering her expression when she saw my face. *My scar.* She only saw that one, but that was enough. My injuries were the reason I didn't come home when I was supposed to.

It was meant to be one of the last missions. After the initial deployment, I—together with a handful of others—got extended to *clean up*. Our specialty. But it all went to shit when the intel proved to be wrong. Was it wrong, though? Or did someone else pull the strings? At that point, nothing was a surprise.

I walked into the building, expecting two targets. Spending all night doing recon of the area, there was no indication otherwise. It should've been as easy as when Davis and I were fourteen and used his father's liquor stash for target practice.

In the end, nothing went as planned. Instead of two, there were six. I got three before they had me pinned down. One of those crazy motherfuckers got lucky. He nearly gutted me, followed by stabbing me in the kidney. Losing blood like a running faucet, they managed to overpower me. One had a machete-size knife near my face when an explosion nearby served as the distraction I needed. Unfortunately, his blade nearly took my face off. Falling back on good old adrenaline and my reason to live, I would not die in that shithole. I was going to go home. To Lou. But adrenaline only takes you so far if you lose too much blood too fast.

I survived, only to learn that the world I left over a year ago no longer existed. But neither did I. To everyone's knowledge, George Weiler had become a ghost when the bombs went off in that village halfway around the world.

. . .

THE MORNING after Lou and I spent the night together, I went straight to my father.

Entering his penthouse office, the muscles in my neck and shoulders were so coiled I could barely move my head. There was always a chance he would deny my request, especially if Lee wasn't on our side. Lee was younger than Father and Davis's old man but older than me—a generation in between. He was the head of the third leading family.

"George." Father's brows arched when I settled in the chair across from his desk. "I didn't expect you home until next week."

"Something came up." My nails dug into the wooden armrests. Leaving Lou at her condo went against every fiber of my being, and I fought the urge to turn around several times.

Raymond Weiler was dubbed "marble statue" for a reason—he didn't show his cards. Angling his head, no muscle in his face moved. He was waiting.

"Were you aware of what was happening to Lou for the last week and a half?" I didn't know what I'd have done if he was.

"What is your association with Eloise Cartwright?" He folded his hands on top of the desk. Lou was Penny's friend.

Hearing her full name out of his mouth sent a flush of heat through me. It wouldn't show on my face. I didn't have to worry about that. Our training was extensive growing up. That included controlling our bodies like we controlled our weapons. I cuffed my biceps. "She is my girlfriend."

That got the first genuine reaction. "Is that so?" To the unobserving eye, he hadn't shown any response other than his words, but I saw the tic in his jaw and the slight twitch of his eye. He wanted me to elaborate.

We were under time constraints with my impending return to base and deploying for the next several months. So, I didn't beat around the bush. "I want you to overrule the agreement."

Here went nothing. "I'll step down and become one of the executioners. Penny can take my position. She's better with the business side anyway."

I'll do whatever you want.

I kept my tone neutral, despite my ribs constricting my ability to breathe.

"I don't have the authority to change the ruling, son. You know that." It was a standard answer. A test.

"With Lee, you can. It'll be two against one. It won't matter what Lou's parents want."

My father settled back in his leather chair, mimicking my posture. A small smile tugged on the corner of his mouth. He and Lee had been friends since he became one of the three—a fact that Davis Senior never liked.

"She is special." He didn't phrase it like a question.

"She is." I never expected to find *the one*. In our world, we were paired with someone who complemented us and our branch the best. In Lou's case (and the Institute's), it was the Davis side of *The Order*.

"She is my puzzle piece." I leaned my forearms on my knees, leveling my father.

It was a phrase he always used to describe my mother growing up. My parents were a rare exception. They were contracted like all the leaders' marriages were, but they fell in love.

Silence hovered between us. The only sound in the room was the clock on the wall. With every tick echoing in my ear, my pulse sped up. By the time Father opened his mouth, I was struggling to keep my breath steady.

"I will speak to Lee." Air left me with a whoosh. "Under one condition."

Fuck.

"Name it." My response was too fast, but he let it slide.

"You will continue your military career and strengthen our connections. You are the heir to this chair. While your sister may have a business mindset, she is too soft. Once you take over, you can share responsibilities with her—that will be yours to decide—but until then, I am in charge."

He wasn't done, and while his conditions were reasonable, chills ran down my spine. He was asking me to leave Lou—

"In exchange, I will guarantee Eloise's safety until you return. You have to prove to *The Order* that you can remain a leader with her by your side. Do not let her become your weakness."

"She is not—"

My father held up a hand. "You don't need to convince me. Or even Lee. He will rule in your favor, no questions asked. It's the rest of the families you have to convince. You may have always associated with Marshall, but you are nothing like him. He will fight this. You are taking his *toy* away."

I could feel the muscles in my neck tic. Toy. The term was so degrading, but he was right. Davis wasn't capable of genuine emotions. This would be the end of my friendship.

THE SUV I've been waiting for pulls up. I tighten my hold around the revolver, consciously removing my finger from the trigger. I've come to see what Penny told me with tears streaming down her face.

A guard exits the vehicle's passenger side, sweeping the surroundings before approaching the back door.

My breath stalls as Davis comes into view first. He is dressed in a tux, yet his Silk Cut hangs from his lips. My stomach hardens at his ignorance for—

A hand appears, and Davis helps her out. Her back is to me, her blonde hair tied in an elaborate bun at the nape of her neck.

A Greek-style emerald-green gown makes her appear like the goddess she is.

Mania.

Davis places his hand on her lower back and leans down to her ear. Spots appear in my vision, and I blink away the haze urging me to violence like never before. While I was fighting for survival, Davis stole everything from me. My family, my position in *The Order*, and my love.

As he straightens, Lou peers up, and I see her profile. My heart squeezes as she smiles at *the devil*, nodding to whatever he says.

When he takes a step to the side, Lou turns, and the reason Penny had begged me not to come here tonight comes into view —their son.

Davis moves toward the entrance, but Lou halts. Her spine goes rigid as she cradles the baby with both arms, peering up and down the sidewalk. Suddenly, she glances over her shoulder, and I retreat further into the shadow. Her gaze swipes over the spot I am hiding, and my stomach clenches.

Focusing back on her son, she coos something, stroking his cheek before following her husband inside to present the heir to *The Davis Order*.

Corbin Davis would one day rule everything.

Part Two

The long game.

CHAPTER TWELVE

GEORGE

Present

Time line:

Sometime after I Am the Dark (The Dark Series, Book Six) and Rezoned (The Davis Order Prequel)

"Everyone in place?"

"Yes, and I'm heading there now," Marcus, my second, replies as he holds the door for me to exit the security office.

Passing, I peer down at my phone to confirm we're on time. "Has Ethan arrived?"

"He got in thirty minutes ago."

I redirect my focus and nod.

Marcus holds my gaze, amending. "They're all settling into their suites."

"Good. Tell them I want to see them in the morning." A hyper-awareness I rarely experience anymore slithers through me. I can sense the change of flooring from linoleum to expensive cherry hardwood as we cross the threshold from the employee section to the hallway leading to the ballrooms as if I were barefoot. I've been doing this job for the better part of my life, but officially meeting two of the four *biological* Davis siblings after their adopted brother worked for me for years is a plot twist I didn't expect to happen. Not that they will be aware of my connection to their father.

"Yes, sir." Marcus turns and heads toward the event, passing several of my men lining the walls.

Today is the first time since their original press conference that both owners of the Altman will make a public appearance together. The press has camped outside for days. The event is invite only, yet the vultures, as Rhys always calls them, hope to get a glance at the guests—they won't. Everyone in attendance is either already here or will arrive in the underground garage in one of the hotel's provided vehicles. The Altman Hotels are one of the most secure hotel empires for a reason.

Watching Marcus's retreating form, a memory I've suppressed for nearly three decades, resurfaces.

"I WANT you to work for me." Denton John Altman II leaned against his desk with his arms folded over his chest. I never directly spoke to the man. He wasn't part of *The Order*.

"Why would I work for you?" I sneered at the old man.

His goons had found me in the back alley of his New York hotel, staking out potential entrance points, and dragged me in here at gunpoint. Not that I cared if I lived or died—once I got my revenge.

My life had one singular goal: taking out Marshall Davis.

He had my parents gunned down outside of our home just two weeks after I left for my deployment. He eliminated everyone that didn't fall in line with his plan of being the sole leader. If the Institute couldn't reform them, he had them killed. Not that he gave my parents a chance—Father would've never submitted.

While Penny was spared, Davis made his point by sentencing her to months in a reformation chamber. Having worked for our arm of *The Order*, she was useful. He ensured she'd be loyal to him going forward.

With my mission falling under Yankee White clearance, I didn't find out what was happening back at home until it was too late. The night Penny revealed to me that Lou had married Davis and given him a son was also the night I found out that I was an orphan.

Davis took out my family, Lou's protection, and made her his —as she was originally supposed to be.

It'd been two years since I watched the love of my life walk into this very hotel I was now standing in. I had watched her, made sure that she was safe. *Happy*. It didn't matter that she was a Davis now; her life would forever be tethered to mine—until two weeks ago when I got the call that eliminated the last bit of humanity I managed to hold on to.

Lou had been killed by one of Davis's rivals.

In forty-eight hours, the Altman Hotel was hosting the engagement party for the devil and his psychotic queen. Carolyn Veil finally got what she wanted. If she hadn't had an airtight alibi for Lou's "accident"—as the press labeled it—I would've already killed her.

It was my last chance before Davis moved *his family* south. He'd grown tired of the city and purchased a hundred-acre plantation in Georgia.

"You need resources. Think about it, son. The devil is untouchable."

"No one is untouchable." My fists curled as a wave of heat surged through my body.

Altman stroked his chin with his thumb and forefinger. "Maybe so. But you need to play the long game. Don't act irrational—"

"HE FUCKING KILLED EVERYONE I LOVED!" Spit flew out of my mouth, and I lunged. Arms captured me from behind before I took my first step.

The old man didn't move a muscle. At that moment, he reminded me so much of my father that all fight left me. I sagged against the body restraining me, a hollow void expanding in my chest.

"You haven't lost everyone. Your sister is alive. And she needs you now more than ever."

Razor blades sliced the back of my throat. "What do you want?"

Why would he want me to work for him?

Altman slowly rounded his desk and settled in the high-back leather chair. "Are you aware of how I became connected to *The Order*?"

My silence was answer enough, and he nodded to himself. "Well, let's revisit the past. Shall we?"

He reached toward the corner where a set of tumblers sat with a carafe of amber liquid. Pouring both of us two fingers, he held a glass out. The arms around me disappeared, and I hesitantly reached for the drink.

Altman took a sip. "*The Order* provided the capital for my first hotel." When he noticed my confusion, he elaborated. "Back then, two of the three families lived in Los Angeles before everyone relocated to the East Coast."

Ah.

"In return, I had to open my doors for anything and anyone *The Order* didn't want too close to home. I was given enough money to open several more hotels across the country until I was able to expand on my own. While I didn't need *The Order* anymore, I was tied to it."

He knew too much.

I remained mute, still unsure of where he was going.

"I want you to become my head of security—in time. You have the skills. The connections. But you need to cool this hot head of yours first. Reacquaint yourself with those manners your mother forced on you and your sister with the private schools, etiquette classes, and cotillions. You need to fit in to become invisible."

He chuckled to himself, and I sensed the frown form between my brows.

"You don't need to change your name. No one expects you to come back after what Davis did. He's too self-centered to consider you a threat. But you simply need to disappear until it's time."

"Time for what?"

"To take down *The Order*."

I blinked. My mouth parted, the question of why he would want to take down the devil on my lips.

"He took from me as well. Many of the ones he murdered were my friends. I had to make dishonorable choices to protect what's mine."

"And what do you expect from me? What does your "head of security"—I form air quotes around those three words—"have to do?"

"You will protect my family. My daughter and grandson."

"What about her husband?" I scoff, cuffing my biceps with one hand while holding on to my drink with the other.

Altman pursed his lips but, after a moment of silence, added,

"All of them. While I have an agreement with Marshall Davis, I don't trust him."

"Wise choice." I rolled my eyes.

"He has access to my hotels whenever he wants and continues to get a percentage of my profit as originally agreed upon when I received my loan. The money is automatically transferred to one of his shell corporations. I'm staying out of his way, and he leaves my family alone. They are not to know my connection to *The Davis Order*. And you will ensure that."

Little did I know (or expect) in agreeing to Denton John Altman II's terms, I would have to make many questionable decisions over the years to protect his family. But they had become mine, and I vowed never to let anyone down again.

My cell vibrates in my palm, and I realize I am still rooted in the middle of the hallway. Lifting the device to my line of sight, I read the message from one of my staff members.

Sir, you have a visitor that was not on the guest list. She is waiting at the back entrance.

She?

My mind starts going over who was not invited but could have a motive to want to attend. I come up blank. I had eyes on everyone deemed important or dangerous.

Me: Take her to the motor pool holding cell.

As far away from everyone I care about as possible, yet out of the prying eye of the vultures.

CHAPTER THIRTEEN

GEORGE

ME: I **HAVE TO TAKE CARE OF SOMETHING. T**AKE **POINT
until I get there.**

Marcus: Do you need backup?

Warmth expands behind my ribs. The Altman family was not
the only family I gained by taking this position. Slowly building
my team, most of them having a similar past in one way or
another to mine, has bonded everyone in a unique way.

Me: Remain on standby.

I don't anticipate one singular woman to be of concern, but I
was wrong in that aspect before.

It doesn't take long to reach my destination, yet it feels
longer. The unknown of who could've shown up uninvited sends
a sense of unease through me.

The motor pool doesn't share the elevator bank of the main
hotel for multiple reasons, and I veer back through the hallway
where our security office is located. I briefly contemplate taking

a look. All holding rooms are outfitted with cameras and micro-phones, but curiosity mingling with the suspicion that this visitor would impact today's events compels me to head straight down. I don't want anything to ruin this night.

Exiting the elevator, I spot Jax outside the door in question. My feet slow, unsure as to why the Altman head legal counsel is here instead of with everyone upstairs.

His eyes find mine, and my rib cage constricts. I halt a few feet in front of him.

Jax pinches the bridge of his nose. "You are not going to like this."

Jax is the best at his profession, yet he always has a joke on his lips. His seriousness does not sit well with me. "Explain."

He steps to the side, giving me access to the small window set in the steel door.

I peer at him as I approach the opening. It doesn't escape me how the muscle in his jaw tics. His shoulders are tense, and he is biting the insides of his cheeks.

Slowly, I turn my gaze from Jax to the room. A woman stands with her back to the door. At her posture of crossed arms and wide stance, I deduct readiness. But for what? A fight? Appre-hension? A long, blonde braid hangs down her back, and a famil-iarity I haven't experienced in a long time jolts my core. The woman is dressed in black linen joggers, laced ankle boots, and a fitted cotton shirt in the same color.

My fingers curl around the handle when a hand lands on my shoulder. I don't avert my eyes, and Jax speaks. "I'm out here if you need me."

I nod before pushing the barrier open. She doesn't turn. My earlier apprehension morphs into a blaring alarm ringing in my ears.

"I was told you asked for me by name?" I slant my head, waiting for her to reveal her identity.

Her spine stiffens, and her shoulders rise and fall. "I did."

That voice.

My heart stutters to a halt before taking off in a thrashing rhythm. She turns in slow motion, and her chocolate-brown eyes meet mine.

"Ares." The name is a mere whisper, but she might as well have shouted it.

I recoil, my back hitting the wall. Reality clashes with the past. Flashes of her face underneath me when we— A swarm of... something erupts in my stomach. "Mania," I rasp.

We stare at each other. Time has no meaning. It could've been ten seconds or ten minutes. Not once in my life was I compelled to flee, no matter what the situation was—but this is too much. Lou died over thirty years ago. While I never made peace with it, I accepted it.

"I'm sorry to crash today's events, but it seemed the easiest way to get to you." Lou bites her bottom lip.

More memories begin to flicker in rapid succession. I close my eyes and count to three before I'm able to face her. Lou is more beautiful than ever. It almost hurts to look at her. Her hair is the same shade of blonde. While we both have aged, walked through life, and adapted to fate—or circumstance, whatever you want to call it—my feelings have never faded. I would've done anything for her. Growing up in our world, love was seen as a weakness. Lou had been my strength. Even after I lost her, her ability to evoke feelings in me lived on. I've carried our time together with me through the decades.

"You are dead." The three words are the only thing I manage to verbalize.

She meshes her lips and lowers her gaze before leveling me head-on. "On paper, I am. Yes."

"Why are you here?"

I haven't experienced many moments of helplessness, but

this... standing in front of Eloise Cartwright after mourning her for so long renders me paralyzed. I have questions, yet none of them form.

"It's time to take back what was taken from me. From us." The clouds overshadowing the hardness in her eyes reveal that she has been through a hell of her own in all those years.

My phone buzzes in my pocket, and the vibration echoes in the quiet room.

Lou flicks her eyes in the direction of the interruption. Her ability to catalog her surroundings doesn't escape me.

"Can we talk?" She interlaces her arms behind her back, and my brows rise.

The corner of her mouth twitches, and she lets her arms fall to the sides. "Old habits die hard." Lou shrugs a shoulder.

Old habits. Our training.

My gaze is stuck on her lips. This minuscule, barely there motion triggers an avalanche. It's been so long, but at the same time, it feels like yesterday. The onslaught of emotions contradicts the signals my brain sends. I'm twenty-two again, reliving the moment our eyes locked at *Underground*. Logic gets overwritten by the crippling need to touch her—urging me to confirm that this is not a dream. Or nightmare.

A knock catapults me back to the present. I blink. Lou is already focused on someone behind me. I pivot, finding Jax, his knuckles still near the doorframe where he made himself known.

How did I miss him opening the door?

Jax studies Lou. "Eloise Cartwright."

Lou nods. "Jaxon. It's been...a while."

He ignores the comment and turns to me. "Marcus wants to know if you need backup. You didn't answer his call."

"No, I'm fine." I pause. "He is in charge for tonight. Ethan can help out if needed." I don't have to see Lou to sense the shift in the atmosphere. I mentioned Davis's adopted son on purpose.

"You sure?" This time he scans our surprise visitor.

"Affirmative."

CHAPTER FOURTEEN

LOU

MY HEART STILL THUNDERS AGAINST MY RIBS. THE ABILITY TO take a steady breath has proven a Herculean effort, yet no one would guess.

Growing up, *The Order* set the bar. Many of us failed. I didn't. I became too much of a risk to Marshall when he realized what a Cartwright's mind could do. Which was why the Institute—when he understood he couldn't—was tasked to break me. They failed. Again.

Ever since I've bided my time. Made connections. Perfected my facade. I am in full control of what the onlooker sees.

It had been torture to stand by, unable to interfere. There had been moments I let my grief consume me, resorting to measures to numb the pain—until the night I saw George on TV. My Ares. He was alive. Marshall had lied to me.

I've played tonight's reunion out in my head more times than I can count. I didn't know how it would happen or how long I would have to wait. The right pieces (*players*) to fall into place.

Just being in the same city for the last two days had my insides buzzing with anticipation.

Leaving the holding cell, he led me through a myriad of corridors. It didn't escape me how we never entered the main parts of the hotel. That suited me just fine. I didn't expect anyone to recognize me apart from Jaxon, but I also hadn't been around many people in years and wanted to keep it this way. For now.

We're now in one of the Altman hotel suites. George takes a seat across from me, the coffee table separating us. I could build a brick wall between us, and I would still sense his nearness. The connection we once shared, while dormant for so long, woke up the second I crossed the threshold to the Altman.

The soft couch cushion should be comfortable. Inviting. Instead, my ass might as well be sitting on a bed of needles. Relaxing is an impossibility until all cards are out in the open.

I fold my hands carefully in my lap, waiting for the man I once loved with all my soul—no, love, present tense—to speak.

"How are you alive?" His voice is deeper. The timbre immediately warms my body—a sensation I haven't experienced since...

A chuckle bubbles in my throat. *Nervousness?* How odd. Something I also haven't been privileged to. I forgot how exhilarating this could be. "I could ask you the same thing." My lips curve at the corners, remembering the shock when I saw his face appear on the news a few years ago.

George angles his head, one brow arching in a perfect semicircle.

Heat shoots to my core. I wonder if he's had many relationships.

He waits for me to elaborate.

"Marshall told me you were killed. He showed me your death certificate." Grief snuffs out the warmth, and the night Marshall walked into my room in his house resurfaces from the rubble I buried it under.

"When was that?" The mistrust in George's question is no surprise.

"About two months after you left." My fingers clasp together in a vise grip. "He had pictures. I now understand that they were fake."

"You were already with him." He's not asking. The undertone of anger and hurt bleed into the words.

I lift my chin. "I was at his house. I was not *with* him." I inhale slowly through my nose and hold the oxygen in my lungs until I have to expel it. "I have done many despicable things to survive, Ares, but I never voluntarily betrayed you."

His eyes flash at the name. It slipped out, but it also has never felt more right.

"Then how did Marshall and you conceive Corbin?" This time, he lets his distaste show openly.

Hearing my son's name out of his mouth is like a slap to the face. Not because George feels deceived but because the truth is nothing like what he assumes.

"I will tell you, but... I ask you not to interrupt me. Please. This... I haven't let those memories in in a very long time." I keep my modulation equal, willing the tears that threaten to appear to dry.

George slashes his mouth but then jerks his head in a nod.

The tension keeping my muscles strained melts away at his agreement. I settle into the couch, the grip between my hands loosening. My thumb strokes back and forth along my forefinger, the soothing sensation calming my nerves.

"As you remember, I stayed with your parents after you left. After they were...killed, I had nowhere to go. Car showed up, saying she'd drive me home. My parents were waiting." My heart rate picks up, reliving the day. "I didn't know what to do. Penny wasn't there. I had no money or means to run." I chew on my bottom lip. "I let her take me." My eyes find my hands in my lap. "I should've run. Nic was in the back seat when I got in. Thinking about it later, she was acting weird. But my nerves were all over the place. I was grieving your parents even though I hadn't been with them for long. But they had been more of a family than mine ever was. We were driving when suddenly something covered my face, and I felt a jab in my arm. The next thing I remembered was waking up in a reformation chamber."

Glancing up, George's obsidian irises darken even more. He holds himself eerily still but doesn't interrupt, as I had asked.

"They kept me drugged. It didn't take long, though, before Marshall started visiting. At first, he would just stand next to the door, watch me on the cot, unable to even move. My muscles wouldn't work, yet my mind was sharp. They did to me what I did to the one that needed to be...fixed."

This time, I can't suppress the tears clogging my throat. I swallow several times before I'm able to continue.

"Eventually, he started to move into the cell. He sat next to me, stroking my hair. I remember tears running down my face, and he would just smile at my grief and fear. *'You will be mine soon enough. You will give me the heir I was meant to have,'*" I repeat the words he whispered in my ear the day before he came back and—

I lift my head and stare at George head-on. I don't speak the words. I don't have to. The vein in his neck throbs, and he blinks his eyes closed.

"Did he hurt you?" He forces the question out between his teeth.

Hollowing my cheeks, I think about my reply. "I was too numb to feel it." The truth.

George shoots out of his seat and stalks to the window, his hands interlaced on the top of his head. He watches the city outside, and I know I have to give him the time he needs to process, to rein in his temper. He isn't the same man he was back then, but I just gave him one more reason to help me.

Turning, he levels me. "You married him to protect yourself."

I press the tip of my tongue against my teeth, not wanting to smile. He will always know me like no other.

"I did." I take a deep breath. "I was pregnant. I stayed in one of his guest rooms at first. I refused to sleep in the same bed as him. But I knew I had to protect the baby." I slowly stand, unable to sit still anymore. "Then, one day, he came home with your death certificate. He said it had been delivered to Penny." My voice cracks. "I hadn't seen her since— And I— I didn't—"

George takes a step toward me, and I suck in a breath. He is still several feet away, yet his nearness envelops me.

"You don't have to explain further. I understand." His chest rises and falls before he continues. "When he showed you the death certificate, I was still on deployment. I had no idea what was going on at home until I came back months later. I was extended and then—" He gestures at his face—the scar that expands from his forehead diagonally across down to his cheek.

"You were injured," I breathe.

"Yes. I woke up in a local hospital. They patched me up as good as they could, but no one spoke English. It took months for me to heal enough to travel to the closest embassy. I had no passport, no identification. It was...challenging to get back."

He is not telling me everything, but he doesn't need to. It's no longer important.

"When I got back, Penny told me what happened. I didn't believe her and had to see for myself."

A sharp pain punctures my heart. "You were there. At the Altman."

George peers at the ceiling. "I was."

My hand flies to my chest. "I thought I had imagined it. I felt you." I shake my head. "It sounds ridiculous, I know—"

He waves me off, taking one step closer. Electricity crackles in the air.

"But I was too late. It appeared to me that you wanted to be there."

A cold sadness settles behind my ribs. "I never wanted to be there. Everything I did was to protect Corbin from Marshall."

"Then what happened?"

CHAPTER FIFTEEN

GEORGE

Lou's composure is like no other. She has been in full control this entire time—until now. I watch her throat bob and her brown eyes become dull.

I haven't seen this woman in decades. I mourned her death. I hadn't allowed myself to connect with anyone after being informed that she'd been killed until I started working for Altman's grandson. He was the first to slowly chip away at my steel-fortified armor. I began to care again. Then, I met his family. Things slowly began to change. While still keeping my distance and never letting anyone in all the way, I slowly regained the ability to feel.

Seeing Lou, my Mania, so strong and yet so vulnerable, I fight the urge to wrap her in my arms. This could all be an elaborate scheme. She could be playing me. But even as the thought enters my mind, it already disintegrates.

Eloise Cartwright may have done things to survive, but she would never betray me.

I gesture to the couch she previously occupied. Hesitating at first, she sits down, and I make the split-second decision to settle beside her.

Her eyes widen, but then a calmness overtakes her features.

"What happened next?"

"My facade began to slip." Lou stares at the wall opposite the couch. "Marshall became cruel—more than he already was. With each shred of power he gained, he shed more of his humanity. He talked about how Corbin would reign over *The Davis Order* one day. He purchased land in Georgia, planned on building a compound where he could train him and his other future children. I told him I would never give him any children." She pauses, drawing in a shuddering breath. "Not voluntarily."

At the thought of Davis forcing himself on her, adrenaline rushes my every cell. Marshall Davis will die. If there has ever been doubt, it has been eradicated. I don't know when or where, but he—

"I tried to protect him. I didn't want Corbin to be a part of this world." Her tone is barely audible. She flicks her eyes to the side and holds my gaze. A lone tear escapes and trails down her cheek. "He was small. So kind. He felt so deeply for his young age. The training we went through as kids...it would've broken him."

"Davis faked your death to silence you." The logic behind my statement makes bile climb in my throat. After all these years, I don't have to think about how *The Order* works. It has been etched into every fiber of my being. I simply covered it up, pretending to be someone else.

"I always slept in Corbin's room—out of fear Marshall would take him. One night, I woke up, and Corbin wasn't next to me. I remember how my heart started racing. I jerked upright in the bed. Marshall sat with him in the rocking chair. I always joked that this kid could sleep on the gun range. Nothing ever woke him." She laughs, but the shaky sound quickly turns into a stifled sob.

Without thinking, I reach out and cover one of her hands with mine. Lou's head jerks in my direction. The sensation of my skin on hers... Until now, I was going along, adapting to the circumstance. But forming this physical connection...having the woman I loved, fought for, and lost sitting in front of me makes everything real.

I squeeze her fingers, signaling for her to continue. I am going to be there from now on, by her side, doing what is necessary. Killing who stands in my way. Our way. No one will ever take Lou from me again.

"Marshall informed me that he would no longer tolerate my attempts to *poison* our son's mind. Corbin Davis was the heir to *The Order*, and there was nothing I could do." Lou stares at something behind me. "I asked if he was going to kill me, and he just laughed in my face. *No, Eloise, death would be too merciful. All you had to do was be mine. I didn't even need your devotion, just your loyalty. And womb. But you couldn't do it. It would always be* him."

Davis realized that, no matter what, Lou would never give up on us. He had lost for the first time in his life.

"He had me taken to the Institute. If I ever contacted my son, he would kill Corbin. I knew he would. Marshall Davis had no soul. Mother told me one day that Car had given birth to twins. Marshall had no reason to keep Corbin alive with two more heirs. I bided my time, played their game until I was able to escape. The longer I was there, the more they slacked with their security. Orderlies talked around me. They would forget to lock my door. But I waited months before making my move."

"The massacre." One of my contacts called me one day about a bloodbath at the Cartwright Institute. But he didn't have many details. Davis had shut everyone down immediately, dealt with it.

A menacing grin spreads over Lou's face, and I return her

expression. Everyone always underestimated her—my Mania.

"I stayed in the shadows. Watched as my son became more and more like Marshall. But one day, I would get my revenge. I had almost given up when I saw you."

My brows shoot up. "Me?"

"During *The Babysitter* press conference," she explains.

Oh.

"You were alive." Lou lifts her free hand, her palm hovering near my face. "I couldn't believe it. And working for the Altmans of all families."

I can sense the warmth of her skin and give in, leaning my face against it.

"That was years ago. Why didn't you come to me then?"

She presses her lips together before answering. "It wasn't time. *The Davis Order* had gotten too strong—even for you and me combined."

"What has changed?" A lot has changed, but what triggered her to seek me out now?

"We are no longer alone in the fight. Marshall's empire has started to crumble, and we are going to tear it down." She leans her forehead to mine. "And bury him under it."

A calm settles in my chest, and I inhale deeply. While my ultimate goal has always been to eliminate Marshall Davis, I never anticipated it to be with Lou by my side.

"Does Corbin know you are alive?"

She blinks slowly. "No. Marshall told him the same lie. I was killed by one of his rivals. Even killed a random Norm to solidify his story."

"I will help you get him back."

"No one betrays *The Order*," Lou whispers.

"Except a Davis," I respond automatically.

Lou had been the first *Davis* (being married to Marshall) to do so, but she hadn't, nor would she be, the last.

This is it for George and Lou's (*main*) story.

You can stop here and skip to the epigraph, *or*,
if you don't mind a small spoilery cliffhanger for
The Davis Order, turn the page for the epilogue.

EPILOGUE

CORBIN

FUTURE

TIME LINE:
During The Davis Order.

"E, explain to me again why *The Ghost* wants to meet." I peer at Ethan out of the corner of my eye.

This whole thing doesn't sit right with me. The last few years have been a complete shit show. Trust has become a rare commodity in my family.

Had it been anyone else, like T or even *The Coldblood*, I would've told them to go fuck themselves. I have other things to worry about than some dude that's been hiding in the shadows for years. I've heard enough about him. Who he works for and that he used to be some badass sniper in his day—before someone turned him into Scarface.

"George has something to tell you," my adopted brother replies.

Can he be more evasive?

I fold my arms over my chest and stare out the window. "How much longer?"

"We're almost there."

Ethan parks in front of a nondescript house in the middle of nowhere. My fingers twitch, and I automatically reach for my gun.

"Chill out." Ethan laughs.

Ever since he got his happily ever after, he's been the guy I grew up with again. He hadn't smiled for a decade and didn't speak to me for just as long—not that I can fault him for what I did to him.

We exit his Bronco, and Ethan approaches the structure with confident strides. The hairs on the nape of my neck stand.

He's not going to double-cross me.

Before he can knock, the door swings open, and a woman appears. The moment our eyes lock, her lips part, and her hand flies to her mouth.

But that is nothing compared to the visceral reaction my body is going through. My heart squeezes before it starts thundering in my chest. Recognition slams into me, and I steady myself against the hood of the SUV.

Everything fades away as I stare at the woman. I remember her. Her face is older, but my memory of her hasn't changed.

"*Mom.*"

The End

for now...

Make sure to turn the page.

Thank you so much for reading **The Ghost**,
the prequel to my series:
The Dark Series
The Davis Order
And (not yet started) *The Glass House Series*

As mentioned in my note at the beginning of the novella, while
The Ghost ends with a HEA for George and Lou, you probably
still have a lot of questions.
I'm sorry (a little) to leave you hanging like this.
Everything will be answered over time. I promise.

**If you are ready to keep reading and dive into my
world(s),** there are several entry points.

Some need to be read in order. Others are complete standalones.

The Dark Series

Find out where George has been until the night Lou comes back
and meet some of *The Davis Order* players in that world.

The Davis Order

Who was next to betray The Order after Lou?

The Glass House Series
(Coming after The Davis Order)
Marshall is not the only Davis who spun off on his own.
His little sister had plans of her own.

Turn the page for **TWO exclusive previews** of
In the Dark (The Dark Series, Book One) and
Rezoned (The Davis Order prequel).

Or scan the below barcode for a brief overview of the books that
make up each of my worlds.

$$\overline{\qquad\qquad}$$

KEEP READING

$$\overline{\qquad\qquad}$$

In the Dark
The Dark Series, Book One

Prologue

HIM

I WALK INTO HER ROOM FOR THE NIGHTLY CHECK, EXPECTING THE *usual crying and pleading to let her go home, but when I open the door and hear nothing, I know something is wrong. I rush to her small form on the bed, calling her name, but she is not responding. I shake her, but she's completely limp in my arms. Checking her pulse, I sigh in relief. She's alive. What have I done? I scoop her up and race outside to my car which, thankfully, is still in the driveway from my earlier errand. Making sure she is secure in the backseat, I break every speed limit to the nearest emergency room. I can't lose her, too. Making sure my hat is low, hood covering my hair and most of my face, I race inside the double doors and nearly throw her at the first nurse I can find. "HELP! HELP HER!"*

Back in the car, I lean my forehead against the steering wheel and try to catch my breath, chanting, "She will be fine. She will be fine. She will be fine. I'll get her back."

Chapter One

LILLY

IT'S MID-NOVEMBER, and everyone is talking about the upcoming Thanksgiving break. Denielle and I sit with Emma and Sloane at our usual lunch table. Our cafeteria is a huge, rectangular hall located in the center of where the three wings of Westbridge High meet. Two sets of double doors lead in from the east and west wings. The south wing is connected via two walkways to the east and west wings. Technically, it is its own building, not a wing, but since it's south of the main complex, everyone calls it the south wing. I'm sure someone put *a lot* of thought into it before making that decision, or it was just the most logical, who knows. The south wing also leads to the parking lot and houses the administration offices, health office, and all of the art-related classrooms—best lighting and all.

Our lunch table is in the heart of the room, next to floor-to-ceiling windows overlooking the outdoor seating area and green space. We have the perfect view of everything and everyone. When I'm not required to pay attention to my friends, I tend to just stare outside at the trees framing the school grounds. We are the only mixed table of gymnasts and cheerleaders. Emma and Sloane are the cheerleaders. Denielle and I are on the school's gymnastics team and train at the local academy during our off-season. The rest of the cheerleaders flock around the far corner table by the east exit, and the rest of the gymnasts are spread over different tables on the west side. It's like an unspoken agreement, but since the four of us have been friends since middle school, we refused to conform to that rule when we entered high school. The jocks claim three of the middle tables and are the center of attention, no matter where in the room you are—you can't miss them. This includes my brother, Rhys, quarterback of the school's football team as well as reigning wrestling champion, and his best friend, Wes.

I'm chewing on my turkey-avocado wrap, tempted to let my gaze wander outside and stop listening to Den going on incessantly about her boyfriend, Charlie. They have been together for two years, and this will be the first time he's coming home since he left for college in August. I peer at my watch—twenty-three minutes and counting. I quietly sigh to myself but try to be a supportive best friend and pay attention. Denielle and I have been friends since my family moved back to Westbridge, Virginia four years ago. We lived here when Dad did his tour at the Pentagon, but he ended up taking command in North Carolina for three years, so we moved again. When he retired from the Marine Corps after twenty-some years, he took a government contractor position. His new job requires him to travel, so he doesn't care where we live. Mom has been a corporate attorney with the same firm for as long as I can remember. She is able to commute between her local office and the firm's main office in Alexandria easily. Living in North Carolina, she had to travel for days at a time, and she never liked leaving us kids for that long—especially when Natty, our little sister, was younger. But it wasn't just that. Both my parents had lived in the Virginia area when they went to school, which was where they met, and a lot of their college friends are still here. Rhys had immediately voted for Westbridge, as you would've thought he'd lost a limb when we left there three years earlier and he had to say goodbye to Wes. The two had been inseparable since Rhys's first day at Westbridge Elementary. My brother had dropped his lunch, and Wes shared his grilled cheese sandwich with him. The bond they formed over two pieces of bread resulted in a lifelong friendship. With so many ties to Virginia, my parents figured moving back was a win-win for everyone. Oh, and of course there is Butler Gymnastics Academy where I had trained for years before we moved.

I've done gymnastics my entire life, so it was a no-brainer to rejoin Butler's as soon as my boxes were unpacked. I kept up with it in North Carolina, but it wasn't the same. Every academy has its individual training method, and I remember being so nervous that I wouldn't make the cut. Denielle took one look at me during my first practice session and flashed me a grin. "I like you. I think we'll be best friends." And that was it. Luckily for us, we also attended the same middle school, and she's been by my side ever since. There was never a question we would compete for spots on the school team as soon as we started high school.

I finish my wrap, and Denielle is coming up on thirty-four minutes. My attention is fading quickly. My mind drifts again, and I remember the second week of our freshman year when Charlie literally ran Denielle over. He was coming out of the cafeteria, late for his next class, and we were about to enter for our lunch period. His head was turned, talking to one of his buddies, when he plowed her down. It was comical; her books went flying, and the contents of his opened backpack went everywhere. Den was about to let him have it when their eyes locked. Both of them just stared at each other, slack-jawed. They went on their first date the following weekend and have been together ever since. They have one of those relationships you only read about—*the perfect couple*. They complement each other in every way: where she is spontaneous and temperamental, he is calculated and level-headed. Even their fights make you want to gag at how perfect they are. Sometimes, I wonder how they make it work. Anyway, Charlie left for college this summer, and they are working their way through a long-distance relationship. So far, it's been going well, but Thanksgiving will be the first time he's been back, and to say Den is excited would be like saying the sun is *kinda* warm.

"He'll regret sending me all these naughty texts and then not acting on them."

Emma and Sloane laugh at Denielle's comment, and I just roll my eyes. "You are so full of it. First of all, how could he act on it, being three states away? And second, the minute you two are alone, you'll jump his bones."

Den grins at me sideways. "Wasn't that what I was referring to?"

I just shake my head and gather my things. "Grab your stuff. I don't want to be late for journalism again. Mr. Davey said we'd get our research assignment today."

"Geek."

"Love you, too. Get your ass moving."

"YOU HAVE until after break to finish your paper. We've talked a lot about the news in the last few weeks—how subjectively things are being presented based on the presenter. I want you to pick a current news topic. It can be anything from economics, politics, even a recent criminal case, and research the entire subject. What is being reported and how is it presented versus what you believe is being left out and why."

Mr. Davey mentioning a criminal case immediately intrigues me. Economics and politics have never really interested me. I'm more a math and computer science kinda girl. Plus, our household is composed of an attorney and a former Marine. Heated discussions over politics are a given, which is a reason I stay clear of it as much as I can. Criminal case it is.

RHYS

I GLANCE toward the table by the windows where Lilly and her friends had taken up residence during the first week of freshman year. As much as the three middle tables are ours, that one is *property* of Denielle, Sloane, Emma, and Lilly, with the occasional visit from a random student. Lilly is staring out the window while Sloane and Emma hang on Denielle's every word. I press my lips together to hide the smile that wants to creep across my face from seeing Lilly's bored expression. I wonder what the topic of Den's monologue is that evokes such an opposite reaction in Lilly versus her two friends. Not that I would ever dare ask. If I did, the answer wouldn't extend beyond Denielle's middle finger. Turning back to my table, a chuckle escapes me at the visual in my mind, and Wes gives me *the eyebrow*. Purposefully ignoring my best friend, I shove another forkful of the disgusting *and* cold spaghetti in my mouth. How the cafeteria folks can fuck up something simple like spaghetti is beyond me.

The last two classes are dragging. All I can think about is today's practice since Coach decided to jam extra sessions in before break. I walk between Wes and Jager toward the gym when my girlfriend appears in front of us. Kat gives my friends her usual sultry eye flutter before she wraps her arm around mine and pulls me toward the guys' bathroom we just passed.

"Excuse us, guys. I need Rhys to take care of something for me *really* quick."

She gives me a sidelong glance, and I know exactly what goes through my best friend's and teammate's heads.

Awesome.

Wes fist bumps me as I'm being dragged away, and Jager hoots loudly. However, before we get to the bathroom door, I stumble into someone, which is followed by, "What the fuck, McGuire?"

This is getting better by the minute.

I turn toward the voice and come nose to nose with Lilly's best friend and *my* archenemy. With her four-inch heels, Denielle is almost at eye level with me, and we stare at each other—neither of us budging. I put my most bored expression on, one I have mastered over the last few years, but before I can say anything, Kat sneers from my side, "Watch where you're going. You're holding us up."

Kat intimidates ninety-nine percent of the school's female population, but not Denielle Keller. She just raises an eyebrow and looks between her and me before settling on Kat.

"Oh, you mean now you have to finish him off in three minutes versus five?" Her gaze travels to me, and with a smirk, she continues, "I think you'll be fine. From what I've heard, you two never need more than two."

Instead of walking around me, she bumps her shoulder into mine with as much force as she's able to gather in the short distance between us.

As I follow Den's retreating form, a hiss comes from Kat that sounds something along the lines of *bitch*, but instead of engaging, Den just flips her the finger and keeps walking. I bite the inside of my cheek not to burst out laughing and let Kat drag me the rest of the way into the bathroom.

After ensuring we're alone, she rounds on me. "You've been ignoring me this week."

She can't be serious.

This time, I don't even have to pretend to be bored. "What are you talking about?"

"During lunch *and* practice!" With both fists on her hips, all that's missing is her stomping a foot to complete the temper tantrum.

The urge to turn and walk out is overpowering, but after a calming inhale and exhale, I simply say, "I've had extra practice, and you know that. What do you want from me? Walk you to the other end of the gym in the middle of everything so that we're seen together?" I almost expect her to say yes, but instead, she switches gears altogether.

"Don't forget Emma's party on Friday. I expect you to be there."

It's not like I have anywhere else to be—like home.

"I will."

My answer pacifies her, and she presses a quick kiss on my cheek. "That's my boyfriend."

I sigh inwardly. Yes, it is.

Continue reading Lilly & Rhys's story in
In the Dark, The Dark Series, Book One.

—————————

KEEP READING

—————————

Rezoned
The Davis Order Prequel

(Prologue)

ETHAN

Present

SAYING goodbye to my foster sister is never easy. It makes my chest constrict as much as my (in her presence, permanently coiled) muscles relax. I care for Jenn, love her—on a nonromantic, platonic level. Out of the four Davis siblings, she's the only one I remained in touch with.

However, over the years, we drifted apart. Our lives don't blend well. I work security for the Altman Hotel empire, and she is *The Cleaner* for one of the biggest organized crime families in the western hemisphere. A family I used to be part of—not that I ever asked for it. Did I want to be out of the foster system? Of course. What five-year-old wouldn't want to belong somewhere? But at what cost? A price I didn't understand until it was too late.

"Can I talk to you for a minute?"

My eyes flick to Jenn, and a sour taste forms on my tongue. As good as she is in her profession, she doesn't possess the mask our brothers wear, which is why she is *The Cleaner*, and the guys execute the jobs. She is about to deliver the news I never wanted to get.

My pulse thrashes in my veins as I follow her to the driver's side of her Bugatti. She studies me, and with every passing second, I fight the urge to latch on to her arms and shake her. I don't want to hear what she has to say, but I don't have a choice.

"He found her." Her tone is level. While she visually can't hide shit, she is a professional in her area of expertise. The groove between her brows contradicts her voice. The sorrow and fear for me are etched across every inch, but no one would know just by hearing her speak.

"How?" I choke on the question.

"By sheer coincidence." She peers over to where my employer and her friends stand but continues her recap. "Cor called just before we got here. He overheard Marshall on the phone with Tony. He was on assignment in Maine and stopped at a diner on the drive back."

My fingers flex and curl as I listen. "Don't tell me she works at a diner." Why would she do that? A vision of her red hair behind the counter flashes in front of my mind's eye.

"Not work. She owns it," Jenn states. "It's all she's ever known. Can you blame her?" Her gaze jumps between my eyes.

"And you're telling me Tony stopped at her diner, of all

places?" This is the most fucked-up coincidence in the history of random occurrences.

Jenn nods, and my hands fly up, fisting the strands of my cropped dark hair. I get ahold of enough to pull, causing a sting that distracts me momentarily from the pit that has been ripped open in my stomach.

"Why didn't Tony eliminate her on the spot?" Not that I'm not glad he didn't, but she should've been dead a decade ago. To Marshall Davis's knowledge, she was.

"Marshall ordered him back to the plantation. He probably wants to figure out what happened before taking action." She chews on her bottom lip.

"Are you going to be okay?" What I'm asking is, *will you be safe?*

"He won't kill me." The corner of her mouth quirks and my snarky little sister is back.

I slant my head, not dignifying her attempt to make light of the situation.

Jenn rolls her eyes and places both hands on my shoulders. "You know Father doesn't tolerate disobedience. That's what started this mess in the first place. But Mother will not allow him to harm me. To him, I wasn't even there."

"Maybe not you, but Corbin was. *I* was. He sent me there to watch Ju—" Saying her name constricts my airways, and I have to pause. "How can he not think we had anything to do with her surviving?"

Her expression softens. "I will call you once I have more details. Cor is working on getting the exact location."

JENN HUGS ME, and despite returning the embrace, I feel nothing. A hollow cold has taken over my body.

They found Jules.

Continue reading Ethan & Jules's story in
Rezoned, The Davis Order Prequel

GLOSSARY

The Order and other players.

The leading families:

Weiler

Raymond Weiler - Leader

George Weiler - Firstborn

Penelope "Penny" Weiler - Second born

Davis

Walter Davis - Leader

Marshall Davis - Firstborn

Abigail Davis - Second born

Corbin Davis - Firstborn, next generation (Book: *Firestarter*)

Ethan Davis - Adopted son, next generation (Book: *Rezoned*)

Samuels

Lee Samuels - Leader

The next level:

Cartwright

Eloise "Lou" Cartwright - Firstborn

***Veil**

Carolyn "Car" Veil - Second born

The Norms:

Nicole "Nic" Cole - *No one (yet)*
Denton John Altman II - Hotel Owner (*The Dark Series*)

The *Dark Series* Players.

Rhys McGuire - Main Character (*The Dark Series Trilogy: In the Dark, Out of the Dark, Of Light and Dark*)
Weston "Wes" Sheats - Friend (Main Character: *Because of the Dark*, Book Four)
Denielle "Den" Keller - Friend (Main Character: *Followed by the Dark*, Book Five)
Marcus Baxter - Bodyguard (First appearance: *Because of the Dark*, Book Four; Main Character: *Followed by the Dark*, Book Five)
Jax - Altman head legal counsel (First appearance: *Because of the Dark*, Book Four)

ACKNOWLEDGMENTS

George's story wasn't meant to be written for quite some time, until one evening when Mary and I chatted about a potential novella and which of my characters it could be about. Suddenly, the pieces started falling into place. George began to talk, and I knew it had to be his story.

Yet, I did not expect <u>this</u>. I did not see his connection to *The Order* coming. This proves once again: ***I don't write my books. My characters do***.

If you read the epilogue, many of you are probably not happy with me for the ending: the open questions and (small) cliffhangers to what's to come. And I am sorry—a little bit. ;-) *Did I mention my characters run the show?* I went back and forth many times about how much to reveal right now, and after several conversations with my team, we agreed that this was George and Lou's story. They would find their way back to one another, get their HEA, and the rest will happen over time. I promise everything will be answered. *The Dark Series* covers several players, and book six, *I Am the Dark*, will connect both series again while answering questions my readers have been waiting on for a few years now. Don't miss out on *his* book.

Did you know you can ask my characters questions and their answers will be posted in my newsletter? Click here if you want to chat with them. You can ask anything. Let's see what they have to say.

To the thank-yous:

My husband: You are my rock. Thank you for always believing in me. I couldn't do this without you.

My daughters: While you are not allowed to read my books, your help when I work on covers or other graphic designs always makes my day.

My family and friends: Thank you for cheering me on and recommending my books all over the world. Your support blows me away.

Mary: George is yours. You claimed him first. Thank you for believing in me and my books. I couldn't do this job without you. Don't ever leave me.

Jim: Twelve years of friendship, two weddings (yours and mine), four kids between both of us and now four books together. Who would've anticipated that over a decade ago when we got placed in cubicles next to each other? Thank you for still being my WH.

Den: *(the real one)* Thank you for lending me your New York expertise and taking pictures of George and Lou all over the city. Love you, babe!

My alphas: Mary D. and Erica. Thank you so so much for reading George's story chapter by chapter, giving me your feedback, and helping me bring Ares and Mania to life.

My betas: Ellie, Tiffany, Jessie, and Mary: This time, I actually stuck to my promise of 25k words. Thank you so much for letting me drop this novella on you on short notice and helping me fine-tune George's story.

Jenn from Jenn Lockwood Editing: Thank you for, once again, making my words clean and pretty. I'm so grateful for you being my editor.

Rosa from My Brother's Editor: Thank you so much for proofing George and Lou's story and ensuring *The Ghost* is ready for the world.

My ARC Readers & Street Team: THANK YOU!! Thank you for reading and reviewing my books before they're out in the wild and spreading the word. I'm blown away by your support and wouldn't be here without you!

And finally, you, my readers: Thank you for reading my words and escaping with me into the world(s) my crazy head cooks up. If this was your introduction to my series, I cannot wait to hear what you think of the rest. If you've been with me for a while, thank you from the bottom of my heart for your trust and support. Seeing you fall in love and like (or dislike) my characters makes me so happy because it means I created something you can identify with in one way or another. I can't wait to give you many more books and to hear what you think about them. My inbox is always open. Don't hesitate to email or message me.

It's finally *HIS* turn. I can't begin to tell you how excited and nervous I am to bring *The Dark Series* to an end. So many questions from so many books (including this one) will be answered in *I Am the Dark*. But let's be honest, it will never end. I will always find a way to bring the characters back. And I have so many plans. (insert the evil devil-looking emoji ;-))

Let's go finish *The Dark Series*.

xoxo
Danah Logan

Born and raised in Germany, Danah moved to the US, where she met her husband, eventually trading downtown Chicago's city life for the northern Rockies.

She can be seen hanging with her twin girls and exploring the outdoors when she's not arguing plot points with the characters in her head.

But it's that exact passion that has produced *The Dark Series* and continues to keep her glued to her laptop, following her dreams.

Scan the below QR code to sign up for Danah's newsletter and be the first to know about her upcoming releases, sales, and new arrivals.

Add me on Facebook
www.facebook.com/authordanahlogan/

Follow me on Instagram
www.instagram.com/authordanahlogan/

Visit my Website for more content
and other places to stalk me
www.authordanahlogan.com

Or scan this second QR code for all the links:

ALSO BY DANAH LOGAN

Scan the barcode below for a complete list of all current <u>and</u> future books—planned, plotted, *but not yet written.*

The Ghost
The Beginning.
A Dark Series and Davis Order Novella.
(George & Lou)

<u>The Dark Series</u>
(This series needs to be read in order. While the romance is standalone for each couple, the suspense plot spans throughout the series. I Am the Dark, book 6, is the only interconnected standalone.)

In the Dark, Book 1
Out of the Dark, Book 2
Of Light and Dark, Book 3

(Lilly and Rhys)
A Dark, New-Adult, Romantic-Suspense Trilogy

Because of the Dark, Book 4
(Wes and King)
A Dark, Hidden-Identity, Romantic-Suspense Novel

Followed by the Dark, Book 5
(Denielle and Marcus)
A Dark, Enemies-to-Lovers, Age-Gap,
Romantic-Suspense Novel

I Am the Dark, Book 6
(HIM)
A Dark, Age-Gap, Romantic-Suspense Novel

<u>The Davis Order</u>
(A series of standalones.)

Rezoned, Prequel
(Ethan)
A Dark, Hate-to-Love, Second-Chance,
Romantic-Suspense Novel

Deadzone, Book 1
(Theo)
A Dark, Age-Gap, Romantic-Suspense Novel

Coldblood, Book 2
(Paycen)
A Dark, Touch-Her-and-You-Die, Romantic-Suspense Novel

Cleaner, Book 3

(Jenn)
A Dark, Why-Choose Romantic-Suspense Novel

Firestarter, Book 4
(Corbin)
A Dark, Enemies-to-Lovers, Romantic-Suspense Novel